Before Egypt

Angelique Conger

I0631774

Copyright

Table of Contents

To my own true love, Jack

Dedication

F or Jack, my own true love.

A Plot

Years later, Egyptus would look back on this time as golden. Everyone in her big extended family got along fairly well. Few fought with others as they remembered the blessings of Jehovah when He brought their grandparents through the flood from both above and beneath the earth.

Egyptus opened the door to the home her parents built on the plains of Shinar and stood on the front stoop, breathing in the brisk morning air. She gazed across the last of the wheat standing in the fields, their heavy heads drooping with ripe grain. The upcoming harvest would require great effort to thresh and clean the wheat before they could use it. The early morning lit the fields, causing them to glow with the promise of food for the coming cold times.

A shiver cascaded from her head to her toes. Although she loved the beauty of the fields covered in snow, she did not like the cold or the difficulty of moving in it. What would it be like to live in a land with no snow? Was there such a place? She could only dream.

Afra, just older than Egyptus, strode through her brother Canaan's door and across the land toward the barn and cows awaiting milking. He carried a bucket of warm water to clean the cows' udders in his hands and draped a cloth over his shoulder so the milk would be clean for the family to drink. As Canaan's second son, he had the responsibility to milk the cows and deliver it to the rest of the extended family.

Egyptus jogged across the grassy field, knowing the lush green she enjoyed would soon dry to a crunchy brown. In her arms, she carried a big blue urn and a clean cloth. When her steps brought her next to Afra, she took his elbow. "Do you need help with the cows?"

Afra shortened his stride to allow Egyptus to walk beside him. "You are up early. Do you not want to sleep longer?"

"When do I sleep longer? I like helping you with the cows. They smell good."

He jerked his head in her direction. His nose wiggled like a rabbit nose. "Good? Cow droppings do not smell good."

"They smell good to me," Egyptus argued. "Cows smell clean, like the grass they eat."

"Good thing I keep them out of the onions," he teased. "Their droppings do not smell clean when they get into the onions or garlic."

"Ugh! That would ruin the milk!"

Afra nodded. "It would not be good for drinking, cheese, or anything else. Even the dogs will not drink milk after the cows have been in the onions and garlic."

"Do cows like onions and garlic?" Egyptus trotted along beside her friend.

She enjoyed spending time with the tall, broad-shouldered Afra and had done so since they were little and she followed the boy two years older than her.

"They eat it as joyfully as they eat anything else. Cows are almost as bad as goats."

"Goats? They eat everything. Cows do not."

"No, but we have to watch to ensure they do not tromp through the fields and eat the onions."

"Good thing we already harvested the onions and garlic." She grinned up at her tall friend.

He chuckled. "I can tease you about liking the smell of cow dung and onions now."

Egyptus loved the sound of Afra's deep laugh. "Not now. I know only wheat grows in our fields. Papa will have us harvesting that soon."

They walked together into the sudden coolness of the shade of the barn. A small shiver shook her.

Afra held the door open for her to enter first. Before entering, he stared at the wheat. "It will not be long before we cut the wheat."

"Have the men cleared the threshing floor of flax?"

Afra grabbed a clean bucket and a stool from near the door. "It is gathered and ready to have the fibers broken down. It is good we have many barns for storing food and fibers."

"And animals," she added, setting her urn near the door where it would stay safe. She took a stool and a bucket for herself.

"Yes, especially the animals. Our animals and our large family would not survive if we did not have many barns and all of us working to prepare for the cold months."

They strode to the milking stalls and called to the cows, who entered the milking area with moos and nudging into Afra's and Egyptus's legs. Their warmth drove away the early morning chill. They washed each cow's udders in the warm water before sitting on the stool to milk her.

The other cows stood nearby, patiently waiting for their turn to have their full udders relieved of milk.

"I can milk more cows than you," Egyptus said, her eyes twinkling as she sat beside her first cow.

"No, I can milk more than you," Afra said from beside his.

"We will see," Egyptus, taunted.

Egyptus expertly milked each cow that stepped into her milking stall, softly murmuring kindnesses to each one. Then, she slapped the cow on the rump to move her along and make space for the next one.

Her bucket filled several times. She carried it to a tall, wide urn near the door and carefully poured the warm liquid in without spilling. The first buckets echoed in the vast cavern of the huge vessel.

Afra emptied his bucket after Egyptus. They hurried back to milking in a friendly competition to see who could fill their bucket more often. In the end, Egyptus's soft murmuring to the cows filled her bucket more often than Afra. She milked two more cows than him and emptied her bucket three more times.

"I win," she crowed as she slapped the last cow on the rump to signal her to step away.

She carried her last bucket, nearly full, and dumped it into her blue urn. The milk sloshed into the urn, nearly filling it to the top. Egyptus put her bucket on the ground, set her hands at the base of her back, and leaned back to stretch. "I am happy we do not have to carry that big urn to each home to share the milk with our families," she groaned. "My back is tired from milking and dumping it into the urn."

Afra set the lid on top of the urn and twisted it closed. "It is good I have strong brothers who will help me deliver it. Thank you for your help. I enjoy racing with you. I enjoy your company. We finish faster than I could if I had milked alone."

"When will Heth join you in milking? He is past old enough." Egyptus raised an eyebrow.

Afra growled. "Heth thinks he is too good to get his hands dirty with cows. He is a thinker and a planner. He only joins the harvest because everyone in the family must. He thinks he can rebuild past family glory."

"Past glory? We have little past, except before Jehovah covered the earth with water. That was a time of wickedness. Why would he want to recover those days?" She stared toward Canaan's house, as if she could see Heth at a desk.

"Who knows what he is thinking? He spends many hours reading through the books Grandpapa and Grandmama brought with them. I do not know what he seeks. Jeb and Amor returned from their hunting trip last night. They will come milk with me in the morning." Afra glanced quickly at Egyptus. "It will sadden me."

"You should be happy your brothers will help you again."

"I will be happy to have them help. But I will miss you. Jeb and Amor brought enough game to feed us through the cold time. The hides will become warm blankets. Papa let them leave because he knows you come help me milk." Afra sighed. "But they have returned and will take their place in the milking barn tomorrow."

Egyptus stared at the young man beside her, surprised that he would miss her.

"Besides," Afra continued. "Mama says you should help your mama inside, learning the womanly ways."

Egyptus jabbed her fists into her hips. "I help Mama inside. I rise before anyone else to help you. You will not allow me in the milking barn anymore?"

"I will. The others may not." He tipped his head to the side and shrugged. "They cannot keep you out, but we have only three milking stalls, stools, and buckets."

"They can try," Egyptus grumbled.

Afra grinned. "I look forward to seeing you tomorrow morning."

"I will be here. But now, I must help Mama with our morning meal. She waits for this milk."

Afra lifted her blue urn into her arms and moved to absorb the weight. "I will see you later. If not, tomorrow?"

Egyptus chuckled. "Of course, later. I must take our milk home. Mama ..." She turned and walked through the open barn door that Afra held for her and carried the milk in the blue urn home.

Afra watched Egyptus until she rounded the corner of her home. He sighed. *Mama is right. Young women should do womanly things, not help milk cows. But I like her working beside me. She urges me to work faster than I would if I were alone. And she has a beautiful smile.*

A grin spread across his face.

"Thinking of Egyptus again?" Jeb teased as he and Amor joined him at the milking barn.

"And if I was?" Afra said, turning to his younger brother with a raised fist. His younger brothers knew how to annoy him. His younger brothers still needed to look up to him, but they loved to tease him.

"It would be good," Amor said, lifting a hand to placate his brother. Afra dropped his fist. "Yes. It is good."

Afra and Amor walked into the barn to prepare the low cart with the huge urn filled with milk to be dragged out through the wide doors. While they attached the harness to the cart with grunts and groans, Jeb rushed away to get the team of oxen to pull the cart. Then Amor and Afra attached the yoke to the wagon and loaded the urn of milk.

When Jeb returned with the oxen, the cart was ready. He directed the animals to the front of the wagon, helped set the yoke over their shoulders, and hooked them into the lines.

The oxen dragged the cart slowly through the big doors and moved along the path toward Grandpapa Ham's home.

"Egyptus already took them milk," Afra said.

"One less stop for us," Jeb replied. "When are you going to marry that girl?"

"Egyptus?" Afra stared at his grandparents' home. "She is the daughter of our grandparents, sister to our papa."

"And a beautiful woman you love," Amor said from the other side of the oxen.

Love? Do I love Egyptus? Does she love me? We are friends, but ... can we love each other?

They turned the oxen toward Uncle Phut's home, lumbering down the path.

"Who else would you marry?" Jeb asked. "Not Phut's daughter, Dita? She enjoys her mama's cooking too much."

"And she avoids helping with the harvest," Afra agreed. "No. Not Dita."

BEFORE EGYPT

Amor dipped a bucket into the huge urn and took it to the slab of rock in front of the front door where an empty milk urn waited. He carefully poured the milk into it and hurried back to the cart. Afra and Jeb had urged the oxen to continue moving at a slow, steady pace. Jeb dipped a bucket full of milk and ran to fill an urn on the other side of the path.

"You could marry Mizraim's daughter, Yael," Jeb suggested.

"She is already betrothed to another," Amor said.

"Good. I do not like the way she smells," Afra grumbled.

Egyptus smells good, even when she is among the cows, and she likes their fragrance.

As the young men walked with the cart along the path, Afra's brothers suggested young women he could marry.

"Why are you so intent on getting me married?" Afra asked, slightly vexed by their teasing, as they turned a corner in the family compound.

"We want to marry as well, and we must wait for you," Amor replied.

"Who says you must wait for me? Do you have a young woman who will marry you?" Afra asked, staring at his brother. The heavy cart wheel touched his foot before he jerked it out of the way.

Both Jeb and Amor tilted their heads back, sending gales of laughter echoing between the houses.

Afra set his hands on his hips, waiting for his brothers to stop. "So, the cart almost rolled over my foot. Nothing like when you —"

"No, nothing like that," Amor interrupted. "You do not need to remind us of our follies."

"Not the arrow in your leg?" Afra asked, staring at Amor. "Or the time the oxen stood on your foot?" His gaze turned to Jeb.

"Nor any of the other things we have done," Jeb agreed.

The cart moved slowly down the path as they took turns dipping milk to pour into the waiting urns at each house.

"Why should you not marry Egyptus?" Jeb asked.

Afra rubbed the back of his neck, wiping away the sweat brought on by his running milk to the urns. "I have not asked her."

Amor hooted again. "And why not?"

The oxen pulling the cart took many steps before Afra spoke. "I fear she will say no."

"You fear she will say no? To You?" Jeb stared at his brother, scratching his jaw where a scraggly beard grew.

"She rises early many mornings just to be with you," Amor said.

"She loves milking. She told me this morning she loves the way they smell." Afra took his turn to dip milk from the huge container and run it to the urn waiting on the slab.

When he returned, Jeb had another question. "How do you know it is only the cows she loves?"

Afra walked beside the oxen. They had almost completed the circuit around the family's homes. "She is gentle with the cows and always gets more milk from them than I can." He shrugged. "I do not know if she loves me. She likes me. She laughs and accepts my teasing."

"What other young woman will let you tease her?" Amor asked. Jeb helped him tip the urn to its side to dip the last bucket of milk out.

Afra stood with his mouth open, watching. *Other young women do not allow teasing? I never knew. I never tried. Why would I?*

"You think all girls allow teasing like Egyptus does?" Jeb chuckled.

Afra pushed the hair back out of his eyes and gazed toward the sun, now lifted a span above the eastern mountains. "I have not tried to tease other young women."

Jeb and Amor giggled as they backed the oxen into the barn and unhooked the yoke.

"You have not asked," Amor said with a snicker.

"And you do not tease others," Jeb said through his chortle.

"And you fear she will say no," Amor said, setting the yoke and its leashes on the hooks, still snickering.

"Our strong brother is afraid of a woman," Jeb cackled as he led the oxen away.

Amor slapped Afra on the back and walked out of the barn.

Afra stood staring at the cows, smelling Egyptus among them. *Does she love me? How will I know? She does allow my teasing, and seems to like it. I should ask her to marry me. Will Grandpapa allow it? I suppose I should ask him first.*

He left the barn, careful to close the door behind him, then strode across the field toward his home. Mama would have food waiting for them. She would know how he could ask Egyptus's papa. He would ask her.

Egyptus rounded the corner of her mama's home and gazed up into the sky. Heavy, dark rain clouds rimmed the western edge of the valley. They would drop rain on the fields before the end of the day. Papa would want to know.

As she pushed the back door open, Ruth greeted her. "Mama wonders where you have been with the milk."

"I am here." She handed the blue urn filled with milk to her sister. "Do not spill it. I am going to wash the cow from my hands."

Spinning on the balls of her feet, Egyptus rushed out the door before her sister could complain. At the back of the house where Mama kept a deep dish of water for washing, she poured clean, cold water from the urn nearby and dipped the soap into the water. As the cold water touched her warm hands, she shivered and squealed. "Warm water would be nice in the morning."

After rubbing the soap on her hands and setting it aside to wash, she rinsed the soap from her face, hands, and arms before drying on the towel Mama left hanging on the peg.

Glancing up at the clouds once more, Egyptus sucked in a breath. She shivered in anticipation of the coming cold time. In some ways, she loved the cold time of the year better than the heat. Wheat and rye seed would rest beneath the earth, waiting for warmth of the sunshine to signal it to grow again. But they would have most crops harvested and ready to eat, leaving more time to think and to dream.

Not that she would have time to dream often. Mama kept her busy year round. When the cold kept them indoors, the women spun and wove the fibers they had gathered and grown specifically for fabrics or gathered from sheared sheep, goats, and other animals that lived happier in the heat without all the wool and hair they grew.

We are going to be busy today.

She ran through the kitchen door calling, "Mama! Papa! Have you seen the clouds?"

"Clouds?" Papa asked. Even though he had lived many years since they left the ark, Papa's strength and ability to work kept the others in her family running to keep up.

"They are building up along the edge of the valley."

Papa hurried out the door to gaze at the clouds, then returned to his seat at the table. "We must either cut the last of the wheat today and put it in the barn or hope the rain does not destroy it."

Ruth brought the food to the table where Mama and Papa sat.

"How will you decide?" Mama asked.

"I will pray, as always. Jehovah continues to love and bless us."

The four family members knelt around the table, originally built for a much larger family, to pray before eating. Papa led the prayer. At the end, he added, "Please hold the rains back long enough for us to gather in the final crop of wheat, that we may have sufficient food to survive the coming cold weather."

As Egyptus and Ruth pushed off their knees and Papa helped Mama to her feet, her older brothers, Cush and Canaan, burst into the house. Both brothers were born shortly after their parents had left the ark and were more than twenty years older than Egyptus.

"Papa, did you see the clouds?" Cush cried.

"I am glad you are here," Papa said as he sat in his chair. "Egyptus warned me of the clouds earlier. We just prayed about harvesting today. Gather your families. We need everyone to help harvest the wheat and bring it into the barn. I believe Jehovah will hold the rain back until we finish if we work hard and quickly."

"Today?" Canaan asked, standing rigidly near their father.

"In less than a span, as soon as we eat, we will gather at the edge of the first field. Please have all your children who are old enough meet us there to help. Tell Mizraim and Phut as well, Canaan."

Canaan and Cush mumbled their goodbyes as they raced for the door.

"We should eat now," Mama said, spooning eggs onto flat bread and handing one to each person.

Egyptus sipped the warm goodness from her cup while she waited for her food. "Nothing like fresh milk from the cow."

"You are getting too old to be over there in the milking barn with Afra," Mama said.

"You have been talking to Elva," Egyptus said, glaring at her mama. *That is why Afra suggested I should be doing more inside the house.*

"Why?" Mama asked.

"Afra said his brothers would help in the barn tomorrow. His mama does not think I should be milking."

"We have been talking, yes. We often do that. You and Afra are close ..." Mama handed Egyptus her flat bread filled with eggs.

Egyptus took her food. "We are good friends."

"You have been since you were little. However," her mama lifted a finger and pointed, "you are too old to be alone together."

"Your mama is correct," Papa said. "But now is not the time to argue about this. We have wheat to harvest."

Egyptus took a bite of her meal and sighed. With Mama, Papa, and Afra's mama against her, she could not argue.

"But if Jeb and Amor are there, I will not be alone with Afra."

"No, but you have other things to do here in the house. You are seventeen. Time to be a woman, do more womanly chores," Mama said.

Egyptus groaned. She wanted to be to the fields early today. She ate her food as quickly as she could. She had seen the clouds. They needed to get the wheat harvested.

As she pushed her chair back, Mama stopped her. "Egyptus, before you leave, clean the dishes and set them in order. After that, please start a stew and set it on the edge of the fire so we have warm food to eat tonight. I am going to help Mizraim's family get their little ones ready."

Before Egyptus could complain, the others had left the house for the fields, leaving her with all the dirty dishes to clean. Were they plotting against her?

Harvest

B efore Afra could talk to his mama about his problem, his papa
returned to the warm kitchen.

"Papa Ham declared today is the day to harvest the last of the
wheat. Everyone get your scythes and meet us at the edge of the field,"
he bellowed.

Brothers and sisters tumbled from around the house. Afra hurried
to the storage building and stood behind his brothers until he could
grab his scythe.

*Egyptus warned me this morning we would harvest the wheat soon. I
should have listened to her and put my scythe where I could reach it easier.*

Everyone hurried to get their tools and raced toward the wheat
fields, joining others from the other families in their compound. When
Grandpapa Ham put out the call for help with the harvesting, no
one stayed behind unless they were too little. Older children cared for
the little children on the edge of the fields so their mamas would be
available to help as needed.

The women and older children would follow behind the men after
Grandpapa Ham gave the signal to move forward, gathering the
sheaves of wheat into bundles, tying them at one end of the length of
the wheat stalk and standing them up to dry. They would thresh and
winnow the wheat after it dried.

Afra turned, looking for Egyptus behind him. He could not miss
her lithe form. He hoped she would follow him across the fields. But he
did not see her. He slumped as he waited for the signal.

Grandpapa Ham whistled and the men moved forward, swinging their scythes. Afra moved with them, falling into a rhythm with the other men, swinging his scythe out to cut the wheat stalk low. Soon his back hurt from bending, but he continued to the other side.

His thoughts turned to the things his brothers had said that morning. Did Egyptus care for him? Would she marry him? More importantly, would her papa, his grandpapa, allow it?

He had no reason to believe Grandpapa Ham would not allow his youngest child to marry him, except he was the son of Canaan, and Canaan's behavior had lost his family the privilege of using the Holy Priesthood. Papa could still use the privilege, but none of his sons could, especially not those of Canaan's sons and grandsons.

Papa, you should not have been so curious. We desire the rights of the Priesthood, too.

Papa Canaan often did things without thinking. Afra had seen him and often wondered why he did the things he did. Only in the last year, he had left the compound alone with a jug of wine. He rode out with their dog, King, into the wilderness. Mama had not become worried until he had been gone six days. On the seventh morning, she sent Afra and Jeb out to find him.

Afra had feared they would find their papa injured or dead. Instead, he had been relieved when they had traveled for less than a span when Papa and King had ridden toward them.

"What are you doing out here?" Papa had demanded.

"Mama sent us out to find you," Afra had said. "She feared you were injured."

"King would have come back to get you if I had injured myself. Silly woman."

Papa had snorted and brushed past them, riding toward home.

Afra glanced behind him, wondering which woman tied the wheat he cut. Sadly, Egyptus was not there.

Does she care for me? Are the things my brothers said this morning true, or were they teasing me? They have teased me before. Will Egyptus agree to marry me? Who should I ask first, Egyptus or Grandpapa Ham?

He bent to cut the wheat until he reached the other side, about the same time as the other men. They all flopped onto the ground, watching the women finish bundling the wheat. He glanced down the line of women seeking for Egyptus once more.

This time he caught sight of her. She worked farther down the field, close to her mama. She focused on the wheat, as if thinking of something else. Afra could understand that. He had thought about his papa and Egyptus while he cut the wheat.

Is she thinking of me?

He hoped she would see him and join him when they stopped for the midday meal. He would talk to her then. He had to know if she would accept him as her husband.

Egyptus hurried to the wheat field, arriving as her papa signaled for the men to begin cutting. She had hoped to find a place near Afra, but dishes and preparing the stew for the evening meal had slowed her.

When she had mentioned the coming rain and the wheat harvest, Ruth had frowned at her.

"You had to mention that today," Ruth had grumbled. "I planned to finish sewing my new dress today."

"You can sew it tomorrow," Mama had said. "If we do not harvest the wheat, we will have none to eat. None for us. None for your new family."

Ruth groaned and rushed to her sleeping space to put on an older dress.

Egyptus's older brothers and sisters had married years earlier, leaving only her and Ruth, who prepared to wed someday. Her Hayam had been working to build them a home, but was taking his time. Egyptus wondered if he really wanted to marry her sister.

When Cush and Canaan came asking about the coming rain, Ruth had groaned again. When Mama had left to help Mizraim, she had slipped out of the house, leaving Egyptus to clean the kitchen and prepare the stew.

Now Egyptus gathered wheat behind another of her nephews, trying vainly to ignore the smells that erupted from him.

Rather than be angry about it, she thought about a question she had asked long ago, when her brothers and sisters still lived at home.

Young Egyptus sat on a rug near her mama's feet in the warmth and light of the fire, holding a hank of wool her mama had spun across her hands. Mama rolled the wool into a ball to be used on the loom. The family sat together after dinner to work as rain pounded on the roof.

"Mama," Egyptus asked, "why are there no other families here?"

"There are other families. Your uncles and aunts have large families like we do." Mama twisted the yarn into a ball.

"No, Mama. Why are there only uncles and aunts and Grandpapa Noah and Grandmama Imma?"

"We live in a new world," Mama answered without glancing up. "No one is left on the earth except us."

"New world? Was there an old world?"

Egyptus's sisters and brothers gathered closer to listen. They loved Mama's stories, even when they heard them many times before.

"Yes, Egyptus. We once lived in a different place, a place filled with many people. But those people were not willing to obey Jehovah's laws. They chose to follow the Destroyer and his cult gods. They became wicked and vile people who scorned Jehovah's love."

"How could they not see His love in this beautiful world?" Egyptus uttered, looking at the changing leaves on the mountains. She had said the same thing that rainy evening.

BEFORE EGYPT

"I asked the same question many times," Mama had replied. "Jehovah had commanded Grandpapa Noah and his sons to build a great boat, an ark, to carry His people and the animals through the destruction that was to come. He could not send his children to Earth to a life of sin and sorrow. But those people laughed and taunted those of us who believed."

"Did they help Grandpapa build his ark?" Nita asked, stabbing her needle through the ripped seam of a brother's tunic.

"Only his sons and grandsons." A stray tear dripped from the corner of Mama's eye. She took no notice of it. "Through the years, those sons and grandsons listened to the lies. One by one, and sometimes two or three together, they left our home compound to live in the world and joined the others in jeering at your Grandpapa Noah and throwing rotten vegetables at him and any who worked with him. It was a difficult time."

Cush lifted the knife he sharpened and checked the edge. "More difficult than since you arrived here?"

"The two difficulties are not comparable. We had more people around us then, but we could not go out into the village, especially the women. The dangers were too great. Cult priests waited to capture and hold us to stop Papa Noah from building the ark."

"Did they ever capture a woman?" Leah, another older sister, asked as she wove a basket.

"They did. That woman, a wife of a son of Noah, chose to leave with the priests. It happened before I married your papa." Mama glanced toward Papa who sat at his desk, writing.

Papa felt her gaze and looked up, sharing a special smile with her before returning to his work.

"Mama and Papa have always been close," Egypt thought. "I hope I can find a man to marry me who will love me as Papa loves Mama. Maybe Afra? He is a good friend. Mama says your husband should be your friend. No. He has shown no interest in marrying me."

She glanced down the field to where Afra cut the wheat. He had removed his tunic, leaving his legs sheathed in trousers. His firm, sweat-glistening muscles glistened in the sun. She wanted to touch them. None of her brothers had enticed her to touch their muscles as did Afra's on that day.

She shook her head and continued to bundle wheat. Soon, she slipped back into the memory.

"How long did it take to build the ark?" Canaan had asked, *not looking up from his new tool he was carving.*

"Jehovah asked Papa Noah to call the people of the world to repentance while he built the ark. It took many years, close to a hundred, if I remember right."

Phut chipped a chunk of obsidian to create the blanks for arrows. They would need them to hunt meat soon. "Did the people listen to Grandpapa Noah?"

"Do people listen to Grandpapa Noah now?" Egyptus murmured, glancing around at those working on the wheat with her.

"What?" Afra's younger sister, Lili, asked, bundling the wheat in line beside Egyptus.

Egyptus glanced up, unaware she had spoken aloud. "I am sorry. I was thinking."

"About what?" Afra?"

Egyptus's cheeks flushed hot at her thoughts of his muscles. "No. I remembered something else."

"Oh. I thought you would think about Afra. He thinks about you."

"He thinks about me?" Egyptus asked. A fluttering filled her stomach.

"You two are together almost every morning milking. Is that safe?"

"Why would it not be safe?" Her head flinched to the side.

Lili stopped bundling wheat and stood. "You are not that young. Unmarried men and women should not be alone together at your age."

Egyptus stood and glared at Afra's sister. "He ... I would never —"

"No," Lili agreed. "He would never, but others do not know that of you two. It is not wise to be alone with him like you have been."

"Wise?"

"You do not want others thinking badly of you. It could cause you trouble finding a good man to marry you."

"Oh," Egyptus said. She bent back to bundling wheat. Her stomach felt jittery with excitement as her heart beat faster. *But I do not care about those other men. I only want to marry Afra.*

Gathering Sheaves

The warm fragrance of the wheat and the repetition of gathering and binding soon sent Egyptus back to her memories. Mama seldom spoke of her children who lived before the flood. It must have been hard to lose all her children to the jeering crowds who expected Noah and his three sons, who remained faithful, to fail.

Egyptus hoped she would never be called on to leave her children behind because they refused to obey Jehovah's commandments. Could she continue if such terrible events happened to her?

Papa's whistle sounded across the field and Egyptus glanced up. They had crossed the first field. Behind her, sheaves of wheat stood drying in the field. Only three more fields of wheat to harvest.

She stared into the sky. Dark clouds, heavy with rain, crept into the valley. They did not have much time. Papa would give them only a brief break.

She moved closer to where Afra sat, hoping to follow him for the rest of the day. He chatted with his brothers. She hoped he would notice her when they started cutting the wheat again.

"Egyptus!" Mama called not long after she sat on the ground.

"Yes, Mama?"

"Your papa wants you to join with those who are gathering the sheaves of wheat. We cannot lose all this wheat to the rain."

"I thought I would help bundle the next field," Egyptus said, groaning inside.

Mama shook her head. "No. Papa needs you to help get the sheaves in to the barn. If we wait, it may be too late. You work fast. You can encourage the others to move faster."

"Yes, Mama." Egyptus pushed herself from the ground. She glanced toward Afra, who must have seen her, for he walked toward her with a grin.

"Where have you been?" he asked. "I thought you would gather the wheat I cut."

"I arrived late. Mama asked me to clean the kitchen and start a stew before I left home. She does not like to come home to a dirty kitchen. We will be hungry when we finish harvesting today."

"You are a smart woman, thinking ahead like that," Afra said. "Will you follow me now?"

Egyptus dragged her booted toe through the soil. *He thinks I am smart!* "I want to follow you, but Papa asked that I encourage the young women to gather up all the sheaves and carry them to the barn to dry as quickly as possible." She pointed to the sky. "The clouds gather faster than we expected. If we do not work fast, we and our grain will get wet."

"I do not mind the rain. This work warms me," Afra said.

Egyptus glanced at his body, then hurriedly looked to his face. "But it will not be good for the wheat to get wet, now that we are cutting it. It will go bad. I must go."

Egyptus turned and raced into the field. The memory of Afra with his shirt off warmed her cheeks.

She gathered as many sheaves as she could into her arms and hurried across the field to the waiting wagons. Back and forth she loped, encouraging the other women to move faster. They filled the wagon with the sheaves of wheat.

When the wagon filled and lumbered away, an older boy drove another wagon into its place. Egyptus returned to the field, gathering sheaves of wheat and carrying them to the wagon. Soon, they cleared all the wheat from the field and moved on to the second field.

She rushed back and forth, her back still aching from stooping over the wheat.

The men cutting wheat had stopped for a quick break. She wished she could sit next to Afra and share stories. But the sheaves needed gathering.

Before they finished the second field, Papa moved the men and women who had cut and bundled the wheat on to the third field. Egyptus hoped he would allow them to stop for a midday meal, but Papa pointed to the sky.

"We must hurry," Papa called. "The grain must be in the barn before it rains."

Warm sticky air warned of the imminent rain. Egyptus bent to gathering the sheaves even faster.

She glanced at the women on either side of her. "I can gather more sheaves than you," she challenged.

"No," the woman on her right said.

"I am faster," the woman on her left shouted.

Others along the field argued they were faster.

Soon, they ran to gather the sheaves and take them to the wagon.

When they had cleared the third field, Egyptus bent over with her hands on her knees. "I gathered three hundred sheaves," she said through her panting.

Lili barked a short laugh. "I got three hundred ten. I got more than you."

The other women announced the number of bundles they had gathered and taken to the wagon. Lili had won. A younger boy brought a bucket of water and a dipper, offering each woman a drink.

After drinking, Egyptus glanced at the remaining field of wheat. "I can get more than you on this last field. The rain will soak us if we do not hurry."

"I will get more than you again," Lili scoffed. "My arms are longer than yours."

"We will see," another woman said.

"Let us see," Egyptus said. "Go!"

The women rushed into the field and picked up the sheaves. Determined to gather more than Lili, Egyptus worked to carry more sheaves each time than she had in the previous field. Three had been easy, four filled her arms. She could not carry five without dropping some.

Soon, other women and men joined them, bending to convey the precious wheat to the wagons waiting on the sides.

Egyptus lifted the last bundle into her arms and scurried toward the wagons. Men and women ran beside her, arms filled with sheaves of wheat. She threw her sheaves on top of the nearest wagon and sprinted toward the barn, passing full, lumbering wagons.

"Wait for me," Afra called from behind.

Egyptus slowed her stride long enough for him to catch up, then ran again. She wished she dared take his hand. But no. He had not declared an interest in her. Great drops of rain threatened fell.

They reached the barn with the lead wagon. Stopping to catch her breath, Egyptus leaned on the open door.

"No time to rest now," Papa called. "We must get all this wheat into the barn.

Egyptus took a deep, cleansing breath and joined the men and women who emptied the wagon. They set the sheaves in straight lines around the enormous barn, standing them in little tents to allow the air to circulate. After this much work, they did not want the grain to rot.

Afra watched Egyptus throw the last of the sheaves into the wagon and sprint toward the barn. He had hoped she would walk with him to the barn, giving him time to talk with her.

He glanced up at the sky. No wonder she ran. It would rain before they moved all the wheat inside if they did not hurry.

Afra sprinted after Egyptus, calling for her to wait. She slowed long enough for him to catch up, then sped up again. How could he talk to her about becoming his wife? They could not talk about anything while running.

They ran inside the barn as the first wagon entered.

"Can I speak with you later?" Afra asked.

"If I can get away."

Grandpapa Ham shouted before he could say anything more. They needed to carry the wheat into the barn. Afra hoped there would be enough dry air to blow through the wheat to dry it before rot set in. Rot would mean less food and other problems.

Inhaling deeply, Afra set his scythe next to the barn wall and joined the others, grabbing sheaves of wheat and taking them to the empty space on the floor where Egyptus and others were setting them into tents. He dropped his armload onto the floor and sprinted back to the wagons for more. They emptied the wagons as fast as they could, trying to get all the wheat into the barn before the rain fell.

As the last wagon rolled out of the barn, Afra carried some of the last sheaves of wheat onto the floor. He slowed, looking for Egyptus. *Where is she? I thought she would wait for me. I told he I needed to speak with her.* When he found her, she and her mama were walking together out the door.

His brothers followed him out the barn door. When they stepped out the door, blowing rain hit them in the face.

"We got the wheat into the barn in time," Jeb said, slapping his shoulder.

"If we had waited another span, we would not have had enough time," Afra agreed. The stinging rain blew away his words. He ran across the field and down the path to their door. There, he pulled off his drenched tunic off and shook out the rain.

"We could have waited until the rain stopped," Amor said, also removing his tunic and shaking it. "Grandpapa could have waited until it ended. It will not rain all week."

"Are you certain of that?" Afra asked. "The weather is changing. The leaves on the trees in the mountains have turned from green to yellow and red. Will the rain end tonight or even before the end of the week? Grandpapa Ham knows these things."

Amor gazed into the rain. "It is heavy, but it could end in the night."

"And the wheat would have been heavy with water, rotting before we could get them dry," Afra said, kicking off his shoes. "Grandpapa Ham knows best."

His brothers followed his example, taking off their muddy shoes before walking on their mama's clean floors.

"Mama," Jeb called. "Is there something warm to eat?"

Their mama, Elva, pushed aside the curtain that separated her sleeping space from the living space. She eyed their missing tunics and shoes. "I have hot soup cooking. It will be ready to eat by the time you are dry and properly dressed."

"Yes, Mama," the three young men chorused and hurried into their sleeping room.

Afra toweled the rain from his head and opened his clothing chest. He took the first clean tunic from the top and pulled it over his still damp head. He found his comb and dragged it through his heavy dark hair, staring into the small gleaming square of copper they used for a mirror. When his hair looked presentable, he sat on his bed to pull on slippers.

"Are you getting ready to see Egyptus?" Amor teased.

"In this rain?" Afra asked. "No. There was no time or place to talk with her today. Her papa must have suspected something, for he sent her off to gather in the wheat, rather than allow her to follow me to bundle it into sheaves."

"Grandpapa Ham may not want you as a son and grandson," Jeb teased.

"I fear you are correct," Afra said, his face drooping.

"You will never know if you do not ask," Amor said, tossing his damp towel into the basket holding dirty clothing.

Afra stood slowly from his bed. "I cannot talk to him tonight. I cannot go there in the rain and tramp mud and water all over Grandmama Basya's clean floors."

"Why not?" Amor asked. "You have done it before."

"I was not seeking their permission to marry their daughter then."

No More

"You should not spend so much time alone with Afra," Mama told Egyptus again during their evening meal. "Elva and I have discussed this. It is unseemly for an unmarried woman of your age to spend time alone with a young unmarried man. You can no longer help Afra milk when you are alone."

"But Mama," Egyptus cried. "Afra and I have been friends for as long as I can remember."

"You have been friends since you could toddle across the distance between our homes," Mama said. You two played together while Elva and I washed clothing together."

Egyptus pushed her empty bowl toward the center of the table and leaned her elbows on the table. "Why, then, are you refusing me the joy of milking the cows? I love their warmth and their smell. I go to help milk them because I like being with them."

"And having Afra there milking the cows at the same time is an extra benefit," Ruth suggested. "You like his warmth and his smell."

"I like how he helps me. I like to race with him, trying to milk more cows than he does. I enjoy the cows," Egyptus argued. "And I like being with Afra," she added under her breath. She swallowed away the dryness in her mouth.

"Ah ha!" Ruth said. "You like having Afra there with you."

"So what? He is my friend. We already determined that."

Mama gathered the dishes into a stack. "You are not to be alone with Afra. It is not appropriate."

"But," Egyptus spluttered.

"You heard your mama," Papa said from the other side of the table. "It is time you think of becoming a married woman. You are too old to be alone with a man until you are married."

Mama took the dishes and set them in the pan of water. Ruth left the table, hurrying to retrieve the dress she wanted to sew earlier during the day. Egyptus lay her head on the table, fighting back the tears threatening to escape.

"Who do you think wants to marry me?" Egyptus asked. "I am your daughter. Who will have the courage to ask for me?"

"Young men have asked already," Papa answered. "I have not answered them."

Egyptus lifted her head from the table. "Who has asked?"

"Mizraim's oldest, Yehuda."

"He is fat and lazy!" She wrinkled her nose at the thought.

"I know," Papa replied. "That is why I have not given him my approval."

"Who else?" Egyptus demanded, lifting her head.

"Yitro and Zev have both asked, as have Tovia and Gad." Papa counted them on his fingers as he spoke their names.

"Yitro is old. He has children my age. Gad is not many years younger!" Egyptus moaned. "You would not consider them for me?"

"Not unless someone better asks," Papa said.

"And you think Zev is better? He spends his time drinking wine. Tovia is younger than me. Is there not someone better?"

Papa reached across the table and took hers. "I have not agreed with any of these men. I believe there is someone better for you and I will wait. But not for long. You are seventeen, past the age of marriage."

"Ruth is not yet married."

"But she has Hayam and will marry soon."

Egyptus sucked in a deep breath and let it out noisily. "May I pray about this?"

Papa's eyes softened. "Yes, you may. We can pray together with your mama, if you like."

"Yes, Papa. I would like that. Let us pray, then let me consider my choices."

At his signal, Mama dried her hands and joined them, kneeling beside the table. Papa lifted his arms and the two women followed, repeating the words he used in his prayer to Jehovah, asking that the correct man would have the courage to ask for Egypt. He prayed she would have a long and happy marriage, as he and Mama had.

Tears slipped down Egypt's face as she spoke the amen at the end of the prayer. Papa wanted the best man to marry her, not the first one to ask for her. She leapt from her knees and ran to her papa, throwing her arms around him. "Thank you for understanding."

"You may not believe it, but I know what it is like to want the right person to marry. I struggled with my family to accept your mama. She was different, coming from the east from lands held by Cain and his family."

"I had to prove I knew and loved Jehovah. They did not want to believe it possible for one from those lands to follow and believe Jehovah," Mama said, barely above a whisper. "It was not easy. The correct young man will come to your papa and ask to marry you. I hope he does not wait too long."

Through the rest of the evening and night, the words of her parents swirled through Egypt's head. The correct young man needed to come to papa soon. Who would that be?

Afra, do you love me like I care for you? Please, come speak to Papa.

Early the next morning, Egypt threw a cloak over her head and followed Afra and his brothers to the milking barn in the rain. Carrying her blue milk urn under her arm and her cleaning cloth over her shoulder, she slipped through the milking barn door behind the men.

This morning was like most other mornings, except Jeb and Amor walked beside Afra, laughing and joking. She wanted to walk beside him. Why did Mama and Elva have to interfere?

She followed the men who picked up a bucket and stool from beside the door and marched to a stall. As usual, the cows gathered around, waiting for the men to milk them. They did not care who milked them, as long as someone expressed the milk from their udders.

Afra turned and saw Egyptus and shrugged. "I told you," he whispered.

"Yes, and I told you I would come anyway."

The men had all the milking stools. They dipped their cloths into the bucket of warm water Amor had carried, washed the udders of the first cow that came to their stall and milked it.

Egyptus turned to the wall, seeking another stool and bucket, but the men had taken them all. She shrugged and walked to the bucket and dipped her cloth into the water.

A cow stepped close and pressed her nose against her arm. She rubbed the cow's nose, then stepped back to wash her udders. She set her blue urn in position and rubbed the cow's side.

"There are no stools for me, girl, so I will need to hurry. I apologize," she murmured.

She squatted next to the cow and quickly tugged on her teats, pulling the milk from them. Soon she had stripped all the milk from the cow into her urn standing beneath her on the barn floor, filled now to the top with sweet, warm milk.

Egyptus stood with her urn and patted the cow. "Thank you for your milk. My family will enjoy it."

The cow moved away.

"Enjoy your milking, boys," Egyptus called as she walked to the barn door.

Afra jumped up and ran to the door, a grimace filled his face. "Are you finished already?"

"No way for me to join you. I filled my urn so my family will have milk early today. See you boys later."

"Wait," Afra said.

"I am no longer allowed to be alone with you," Egyptus said, rolling her lips inward. "Papa believes women of my age should be married, not milking cows with their friend."

Rather than allow the tears to fall in front of Afra, she pulled her cloak hood over her head and pushed the door open, hurrying through the rain to her door. She stopped enough to wipe the rain from her face, grateful it had washed away her tears, and slipped off her muddy shoes, and set them by the back door.

Afra saw the joy in Egyptus's eyes fall away when his brothers took all the milking stools, leaving her without one. *I am already milking, or I would give her my stool.*

Later, when he remembered this day, he knew he should have given her his stool. As he milked, he saw her squat near the cow that always came to her, milking it directly into her blue urn. When the cow walked away, Egyptus threw her cloak around her and lifted the urn into her arms.

"See you boys later."

"Wait!" he said, wanting to speak more to her. He had not expected her to leave so soon. *What did I do?*

"Papa will not allow me to be alone with you," Egyptus said. He saw tears well up in her eyes. "He believes women of my age should marry, not milk cows with their friend."

She jerked the hood of her cloak over her head and shoved the door open with her hip, marching out into the rain. Wind caught the door, and Afra grabbed it before it blew open and banged against the wall.

He watched her march toward her home, hunched against the rain. Was she crying?

Now what was he to do?

When he returned to milking, he refused to respond to the taunts and teasing of his brothers. A sickening feeling filled his stomach. Egyptus's papa would not allow her to come help with the milking. She could no longer spend time alone with him. How could he ask her to marry him if her papa refused to allow them to spend time together?

With the three men milking, they finished sooner than he and Egyptus had the day before. Jeb pulled on his cloak and flipped the hood over his head as he stepped out the barn door to get the oxen while Amor and Afra prepared the urn and cart to deliver the milk.

"Who!" Jeb cried.

Afra roused from his misery to go with Amor to the door.

"The rain stopped. Look at the rainbow," Jeb said. "Maybe we could have harvested today after all."

"No. The wheat would have washed to the ground by that heavy rain," Amor said. He elbowed Afra in the ribs. "Grandpapa Ham knows what he is doing."

"He always does," Afra agreed.

He accepted his brother's usual teasing about Egyptus as the oxen pulled the cart through the mud to deliver milk to all the families' homes.

"Egyptus will not want you if she sees you with all that mud splashed on your legs and tunic," Amor teased.

"Mama will not like to see us this muddy either," Afra retorted. "I get the first bath."

"What makes you think she will make us take a bath?" Jeb asked, returning from delivering milk to a home.

"Do you believe she will allow you into her house as you are?" Afra asked.

"Muddy? Me?" Jeb asked, then chuckled.

"No," Amor snickered. "You are not muddy at all. You have suddenly become a darker brown the shade of mud."

"I have new brown trousers," Jeb said.

Soon the three young men were laughing as they carried milk and poured it into the urns waiting by each front door.

They came around the last corner and backed the cart into the barn. Jeb took the oxen to clean the mud off them while Amor and Afra cleaned mud from the huge urn and splashed water on the muddy cart.

"The wheels will move better tomorrow," Amor said.

"True," Afra agreed. "Now we need to wash the mud off us."

"I get the first bath," Amor said, running ahead of his brother.

"Not if I get there first," Afra shouted, chasing after him.

They raced around their house in time to see Jeb step into the wash tub.

"I said I get the first bath," Afra said, standing with his fists on his hips.

"You two were too slow," Jeb taunted, splashing water toward them.

"Did you get both oxen clean?" Amor asked.

"Yes. I waded them through the stream on the way back to their stall. It washed away most of the mud."

"Unfair!" Amor shouted.

"Only because you did not think about it," Jeb said. "Have fun waiting for me to get clean."

Afra shivered in the cool morning air before Jeb finished and his sisters brought out more warm water for his bath. He grumbled at Jeb's prank. *I told him I got the first bath. It is my right as oldest. Jeb will be sorry.*

"Mama is saving food for you two," Lili said. "She is happy you are not bringing mud onto her clean floors. You should hurry, though. We are leaving soon."

"Where are we going?" Afra asked, wishing she would leave so he could bathe.

"We women, not you boys. Today is our day to visit Grandmama Imma."

"Are all of the women going there?"

Lili flipped her hair behind her ear. "We always do. Hurry." She walked back into the house.

Afra stripped his muddy clothing off and dropped it on the ground beside the tub before stepping in. He closed his mouth and sank into the water over his head.

He came up blowing water out of his mouth, then grabbed the cloth and washed away the mud before stepping out and dumping the water from the tub.

Wrapping the towel Lili left for him around himself, he hurried into the house. "Amor will need more water," he called as he rushed past the cooking area to his sleeping space.

"Get dressed fast," Mama called. "Your food is getting cold."

Afra pulled on clean clothes and dragged his fingers through his hair before speeding back to the eating area.

Jeb glanced up from his bowl. "The grains are good. Too bad I ate them all."

"You did not!" Afra cried.

"I would not allow him to eat all the grains," Mama said, setting a bowl filled with steaming hot grains in front of Afra. "I have enough for Amor as well. You should eat. Your papa will need you today."

A lump filled his throat, making it hard to eat. *But I wanted to talk to Egyptus today.*

"You are home early," Ruth said from the fire, where she prepared the family's morning meal.

"Afra's brothers are there helping him milk. There is no room for me. My favorite cow allowed me to milk her, then I came home."

34

"Good. You can cook these grains. I have other things to do this morning." Ruth left the cooking space.

"Ruth?" Egyptus said to her sister's retreating back. "Where are you going?"

Ruth lifted a hand and waved it toward Egyptus. "I will return when the grains are cooked. Do not burn them."

Egyptus set the milk on the table and hurried to the fire and pulled the pot of grains from the fire. She grabbed the long-handled wooden spoon and stirred.

"Oh, Ruth," she muttered.

While the grains cooked, she retrieved bowls and cups from the shelf and spoons from the basket, then set them on the table, stopping by the fire frequently to stir the grains.

She removed the pot of grains as Mama, Papa, and Ruth entered the kitchen.

"Just in time," she said. "The grains are ready to eat."

"Did you make the flat bread to go with the grains?" Mama asked.

"N ... No. No one told me I needed to, and I did not have time. I did not know I should make it," Egyptus stammered, glancing at her mama and papa. "I did bring home the morning milk."

Ruth and Papa could not hold their faces still. They grinned.

"I am teasing, Egyptus," Mama said. "We knew you would not have time for flat bread in the time to cook the grains. But tomorrow," she glanced at Papa and Ruth, "we will expect flat bread with our morning meal."

"I am the cook now?" Egyptus squeaked, unsure if she wanted to cheer or cry.

"For the morning meal. Ruth has moved to the evening meal until she marries. I will continue to cook the midday meal," Mama said as she sat in her chair.

"But ... But how will we have fresh, warm milk to drink if I do not go milk at least one cow?"

"We will have to wait for Afra and his brothers to bring it to us, like all the others in the family," Papa said as he reached across the table for Mama's hand.

Egyptus sighed. *I like the cows. My favorite will not give as much to those men.*

"Did you see the rainbow this morning?" Papa asked as Egyptus dipped grains into his bowl.

"No. It was still raining as I hurried from the milking barn," Egyptus said as she set Papa's bowl in front of him, then dishing up a bowl full of grains for her mama.

"The rain stopped, leaving a big, beautiful one. Too bad you missed it," Ruth teased taking the spoon from Egyptus. "I can dish up my own grains."

"Yes, you are able, but it is my responsibility as morning cook." Egyptus took the spoon back and ladled grains into her sister's bowl. "And you are correct. I should have turned to look up. I need to be more aware, although rainbows seldom happen while it rains."

"You saw the clouds building yesterday. Thank you," Papa said. "Because you did, we harvested the last of the wheat before the rain fell and washed the grain from their heads. But now we can go to the barn and winnow it."

"Today?" Egyptus asked, dipping grains into her bowl and set the pot in the center of the table. Afra's laughing face flashed through her mind.

Papa grinned at her. "Not today. You girls and mama have other things to do today. However, soon the grain will have dried enough to thresh and winnow so we can store it."

"What do we have to do today, Mama? Anything different from other days?" Egyptus sat back in her seat and lifted her spoon.

"We are going to visit your Grandmama Imma today."

"Today?" Ruth asked with a groan. "I thought I would have time to weave. I have much to do before my marriage. When we go to Grandmama Imma's, we spend all day with the other women.

"It is good to be with other women. That is how you learn to be a woman, a wife, and a daughter of Jehovah."

"Is that not what your name means, Mama?" Egyptus asked as she pushed a spoon full of grains into her mouth.

"Egyptus!" Mama cried. "We thank Jehovah for our food before we eat."

"Yes, Mama." She slid from her chair and knelt next to it, raising her hands, prepared to follow her papa's lead, hoping the heat in her face would dissipate before the end of the prayer.

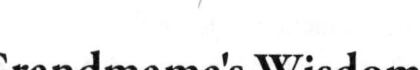

Grandmama's Wisdom

Egyptus and Ruth cleaned the kitchen before they put on their best dresses. Ruth grumbled as they joined Mama to walk to the center of the huge plains of Shinar where Grandmama Imma lived with Grandpapa Noah in a house smaller than all the others.

When they had found this plain, Grandpapa Noah divided the land among his three sons, keeping a small plot of land in the center for his home, worshiping space, barns, and garden. All the sons shared from their fields with their parents.

"I do not like joining all the women of the valley," Ruth whined. "They treat me badly."

"They treat us well enough," Mama said with a little grimace. "Look. Your sisters join us."

Leah, Abigayil, and Dodi strode toward them, grasping the hands of their young daughters. Both Leah and Abigayil carried a babe in her arms.

"You are joining us, Ruth?" Leah teased.

"I always attend, if I am not ill," Ruth retorted. "You know Mama expects all of us to be there. All those women together in one room make me nervous. They talk at the same time, and soon it sounds like chickens in the henhouse." She imitated the chickens. "Bak-bak-bak-bak-bak."

Abigayil giggled. "It does. But when Grandmama stops the gabbling, she has words of wisdom for us. She has lived longer than any of us."

"Not longer than Grandpapa," Ruth said.

"No, but she is the oldest woman," Mama said. "Her name has great meaning for us."

"I had not heard the meaning of Grandmama's name," Dodi said. "Has she shared it with us before?"

"Name meanings are something we keep within as sacred and special. Grandmama's name is sacred. Perhaps if you ask, she will share the meaning of her name today."

"Her stories are always interesting," Leah said.

"She has lived an interesting life. I know the truth of many of her stories," Mama said. "I lived them with her."

"Why must we go with all the other women of the family each month?" Ruth whined. "There are so many of us, we end up sitting near the back where we cannot hear."

"We could sit nearer the front if you would stop complaining and walk faster," Abigayil said.

Ruth, you whine so much, it is no wonder Hayam takes so long to build your home.

The women moved faster and soon entered their grandmama's home. They joined the women from other families inside the home that somehow expanded to hold them all. This many women could not fit into the room if they all sat on chairs, so most brought small cushions to sit on.

"Basya, sit up here. You and your sisters do not need to sit on the floor," Grandmama Imma called. She had braided her white hair and tied it behind her wrinkled head. Old as she was, her strong voice stunned Egyptus once more.

Egyptus and Ruth clung to their mama's hands as she pushed her way through the crowd to the seat Grandmama indicated. Those who sat nearest the chairs made room for Egyptus and Ruth, speaking low enough neither Grandmama nor Mama could hear, but Egyptus and Ruth could. Ruth bristled at their words.

"They are not worth your anger," Egyptus whispered in Ruth's ear, knowing the other young women could hear.

Ruth breathed in and out slowly, calming her frustration. "You are correct, sister," she said when her breathing settled. "These women do not know what they speak of." She turned her face away from the offensive young woman and toward their Grandmama.

Leah and the others found a place to sit with the other wives. They had married sons of both Japheth and Shem. Ham's sons, their brothers, had also found wives from among these families. It had been necessary. In Grandpapa Noah's eyes, all were the same. All were his children and grandchildren.

The youngest girls ran along the edges of the room, shouting and playing together. Grandmama Imma allowed the gabble of visiting to continue for a time, much longer than Egyptus liked. She and Ruth sat together, alone among so many women.

Egyptus remembered playing with her friends in her younger days. Back then, there were not as many women gathered to hear from Grandmama Imma. However, Ruth had never played with the girls her age. She had always been a sober child, sticking close to Mama. It made these monthly gatherings difficult for Mama and now Egyptus.

Normally, Egyptus would find her friends among the other young women her age. But today, Ruth's complaints kept her close. Besides, she rarely had the opportunity to sit so close to Grandmama Imma during these gatherings. And Dodi was correct. Grandmama's stories were interesting and filled with wisdom.

"What do you think she will share with us today?" Egyptus asked Ruth.

"She will read from the life of one of the matriarchs," a young woman near them said. "I saw her carry in a book."

"Are you certain it is not the Book of Commandments?" someone else asked.

"It could be. They all look the same. But the way Grandmama cradled the book differs from how she carries the Book of Commandments."

"Whose story do you think she will share?" Ruth asked.

Egyptus appreciated that her curiosity pushed away her contempt of the other young women.

"I hope she reads from Ganet's story," a young woman sitting behind them said.

Someone mentioned each of the other matriarchs as the best choice by the other young women. Egyptus kept her choice to herself. She loved Eve's story.

"It is hard to tell," Egyptus said. "She has books from all the matriarchs. I have seen them on her shelves. Which one will give her the story to teach the lesson she believes we need? That is the greater question."

The young women sitting near Egyptus agreed.

Grandmama considered it her responsibility to teach all her daughters and granddaughters about Jehovah's love, along with how they could better serve Him.

Egyptus missed the signal from Grandmama to Mama who lifted her arms to call the women to sit quietly and listen. Her face reddened when Mama stared at her, silently expecting her to hush. She listened to the final clucking of discussion, much like the hens in the henhouse Ruth had mocked.

The little ones ran to their mamas like chicks under a hen's wings and all the women settled on their cushions and silently gazed toward Grandmama. Mama nodded to her.

"They should hear you now, Mama."

Egyptus grinned at her mama, calling Grandmama that name.

"We should begin with prayer, as always," Grandmama announced. "Edna, would you lead us?"

Afra followed his mama and sisters part of the way toward Grandmama Imma's home, hoping to see Egyptus. When he finally glimpsed her, she and her sisters had picked up their pace, walking faster. There was no way he could speak to her now.

He trudged slowly back to the barn that housed the oxen. They would need to be cleaned and prepared for the threshing. Some of the younger boys would use long poles with wood attached to the end, called threshing rakes, to beat the wheat. These would need to be examined to ensure the end pieces were tight and not about to fly off into the others.

Perhaps his papa would have words of advice for him. He would not tell him yet that the woman he wanted to marry was Egyptus. Papa would laugh and encourage him to look at the daughters of Shem or Japheth. Those girls would make good wives.

But so would Egyptus.

In the barn, Afra joined the men and moved to take down the threshing flails that needed repair. Afra sat close to his papa. After some small talk, he finally worked up the courage to speak to his papa.

"Papa," he said. "How do I ask a man to give me permission to marry his daughter?"

"What a silly question," Papa answered, picking up a thin rope to wrap around the connection of the flail to the pole. "You go to the man and ask him to allow you to marry her."

"Should I take him something to encourage a positive reply?" Afra stopped inspecting his rake and gazed at his papa.

"Bah!" Papa barked. "That is for women. Men speak their minds. We have no need for bribes."

"No. We would not," Afra said. "Is there something I can do to encourage him to say yes?" He set the flail aside and picked up another.

"You could have his daughter plead for you. That often works. It is how we convinced your mama's papa I would make a good husband for her." Papa tied a knot and pulled on the flail to ensure it would not fly off as men beat with it.

"Papa! I did not know," Afra said. He kept his eyes on his flail, swallowing the words of surprise that sprang to his lips.

"And you will not repeat it," Papa said, glaring at Afra.

Afra straightened and returned the stare. "I would not."

"Who would you speak to? Perhaps I can speak to him for you," Papa asked, setting the rake aside and picking up another.

"No, Papa. I am a man. I need to speak with him on my own. I am uncertain the woman will accept me."

"Who is this young woman who would not accept my son?" Papa all but roared. "My sons are worthy of every woman in Shinar."

"She is worthy of me, Papa, but, am I worthy of her?" The end of the flail wobbled against the pole. Afra wrapped the rope around it to stabilize the tool.

Papa set aside his rake. "Japheth's daughters are haughty, thinking they are better than we are."

"I have seen that." Afra continued to work on the rake.

"And Shem's daughters talk to my sons, but few will marry them. They feel special since their papa received the Priesthood. Bah." Papa spat on the dirt floor. "They are no better than we are. I hope you choose one of my brother's daughters. They will not think themselves better than you. We all carry the curse of our mama."

"But Grandmama carries no mark!" Afra stopped to star at his papa. *None that I have ever seen.*

"No? She came from a family that lived in Cain's land. But her mark has faded."

"But she taught us to love Jehovah," Afra argued.

43

"And she loves Jehovah. She tells of living in a small community on the edge of Cain's land, among a people who followed Jehovah. She claims her family is connected to Adam and Eve. All families did."

"As all families will now connect to Grandpapa Noah and Grandmama Imma. They are the parents of all who live in the world now."

"Yes," Papa said, closely inspecting the rake he held. "And others look down on us as unworthy."

"Because of Grandmama's faded mark?" Afra asked. *Or because of your actions when Grandpapa drank too much wine? I know that is why Jehovah cursed you and your sons. I am cursed because of my papa.*

Papa shrugged. Could he hear Afra's thoughts? He hoped not. He had felt his papa's fist against his chin once when he voiced those opinions in his presence, and watched brothers and uncles receive similar treatment.

"Dunno," Papa mumbled. "Perhaps not because of Mama. She is a good woman and loved by everyone here."

As Egyptus lifted her head after the final amen of the prayer, Grandmama lifted the book that sat in her lap. "The wives of the early patriarchs kept a record of their lives in books like this."

The women in the room allowed little noises of excitement to escape. Most had not been close to these books. Few had read from their pages. However, because Mama had a set of all but Imma's record, Egyptus and her sisters had read them all. Egyptus loved to read Eve's story and had read it many times. She hoped Grandmama would read from that book.

Egyptus sank down in her pillow, allowing Grandmama's words to flow around her, watching Eve and Adam struggle to learn how to fight the battle against the Destroyer without becoming like him. Their first children had listened to his flattering words, choosing the Destroyer over Jehovah.

Grandmama Imma lifted her head from reading. "The Destroyer fought to take their children from the beginning."

She stared around the room, taking in each of her granddaughters. "We are in a new world, much like Eve and Adam. We can serve Jehovah and follow his commandments and bring children into a better world than the one we left." Her hands waved toward Edna, Amina, and Mama, the wives of her three sons. "The world we left had become so wicked Jehovah could no longer send children to it, for the Destroyer had taken over the hearts and minds of all but the eight of us. Even our children and grandchildren fell victim to the lies and wickedness."

I did not know Mama and Papa had other children and grandchildren before Cush and Leah. They never speak of them.

Egyptus glanced up to see Mama brush tears from her face. Edna, Shem's wife, and Amina, Japheth's wife, allowed their tears to roll down their faces, letting them drip onto their dresses.

"I hope you never know or understand the difficulty we faced when our children chose to leave behind the safety and teachings of Jehovah for the excitement, danger, and evil of the outer world," Mama whispered.

"We all faced it," Amina added. "All four of us." She swept an arm out, indicating the four women sitting in the front on chairs. "We each had sons and daughters before ..." she bit her lip, "before we came to this world, before you." She pulled a square of linen from the pocket slung across her shoulder and wiped the tears from her face.

"Children, our beautiful children, chose to leave the safety of the ark to be with the men and women of the world," Edna said, scrubbing tears from her face with her hands. "I hope you never experience the pain of watching your children out the window of an ark while they call from the trees and water rises up to ... to ..." Edna gulped, "to take them."

Egyptus swallowed the tears that suddenly sprang into her eyes. *Could I do that? Could I watch my children struggle to live?*

"We had no choice," Grandmama Imma said, once more taking over the narrative. "All children have the right to choose good or evil, light or dark. You, our dear daughters, have the same right. We pray day and night that you will remember what we teach, that you will desire the light over the darkness of the Destroyer and evil." she returned to reading from her book.

Egyptus half listened as she read parts of Eve's story, sharing times when her children chose the Destroyer over Jehovah.

What would I do if my children choose to listen to the Destroyer? I see others in the family who seem to listen to him. They adore that Nimrod. He is a beautiful man and an expert hunter, but he is haughty.

Grandmama had read about Eve's three sons, Benoni, Cain, and Abel. She lifted her head and gazed at her granddaughters. "Death came into our world that day. Not the death of animals, but the violent death of murder."

She turned through pages until she found the place. She ducked her head once more and read about Cain's punishment, a mark.

Grandmama stared at the women in the room. "Jehovah marked Cain to protect him from his brothers' anger. After a time, that mark was no longer needed. If any of you have a mark identifying you as a child of Cain, it has faded. One of our daughters descended from him, but she no longer carries the mark. The curse affects only those who listen to the Destroyer. Do not allow it to affect you."

"How will it affect us?" a woman in the middle of the room asked.

"You will lose the blessings of Jehovah. Then you will find yourself worshiping false gods who drag you into wicked practices. You and your children will lose the blessings. Stay. Close. To. Jehovah." Grandmama stared around the room.

Egyptus glanced at her mama, her eyes falling on a tinge of pink near the neckline of her dress.

Mama? Is it you? How could it be? Your name ... Basya, daughter of God? How can you be a daughter of Cain? Mama had kept this secret well hidden.

Egyptus decided to ask her mama in the privacy of their home. Not now.

"I ask each of you to listen to your parents' teachings. Learn of Jehovah. Follow His commandments. Keep this new world pure and beautiful," Grandmama said.

Diverted

A fra glanced out at the sky as the men checked the last of the threshing rakes. He finished tightening the last rope around the last rake in the pile.

"I have finished these," he said as he stood and stretched.

"Do not be late for dinner," Papa said, gathering the twine to put it away. "Your mama will not be happy."

Afra thought about the last time he was late for dinner. "No. I will not be late. It is not pleasant to have Mama unhappy with me."

His mama had put his plate away and taken his chair from the table. After begging to use a plate, she eventually allowed him a plate, but refused to let him bring the chair back to the table, forcing him to kneel on the floor. He would never be late like that for another meal. Jeb had come close to receiving the same punishment, but had avoided it by slipping into his chair before she could take it away.

Afra hurried from the work shed, hoping to see Egyptus and her sisters returning from Grandmama Imma's home. He hoped to speak with her while they walked home, with others all around them. No one could say they were alone, even if they walked apart from the other women. Her mama and all Egyptus's sisters would be there with them.

As he neared the women who strolled from Grandmama Imma's home, his mama saw him. "Is your papa finished with you for the day?" she asked.

"He is."

"Good. I need you to go to your Uncle Japheth's and get some elderberries. Auntie Amina has extras and told me to send someone to get them today before she gives them to another. I want some elderberry jam."

"Yes, Mama," Afra said, and ran off toward the far side of the valley, hoping to return before Egyptus entered her home for the night. Uncle Japheth and Aunt Amina lived far on the east side of the valley, near the mountains. He would have to run to get there and back before dinner.

As he rushed past the other women, he saw Egyptus watching him. He desperately wanted to stop and talk with her. He needed to speak with her today. He considered stopping long enough to ask, but it would be too long. His mama had assigned him to hurry to his uncle's home. He had no choice. Like all mamas and papas, his expected their sons to obey their mamas. And he did not want to miss his dinner.

He heard Egyptus speak his name as he rushed past. Egyptus spoke his name, but he hurried past so fast he heard nothing more. He hoped her words were kind.

He raced to get Mama's elderberries, but Auntie Amina wanted to visit with him. He fought against his desire to rush away when she started telling a story. He allowed himself a soft sigh, then politely listened to her story.

"That was nice to hear, Auntie, but I ..."

She started another story.

Afra flicked his eyes upward, then focused on listening to her once more.

As she ended her story, she asked, "What will you do if that happens?"

Before he could answer, Auntie Amina started another story. Afra's stomach hardened. He would never get back to Egyptus before she went inside. He would not get dinner if he did not run.

Finally, he lifted the basket of berries and stepped away from her home. "Mama expects me to hurry home with these berries," he said.

Auntie Amina frowned.

"My Orna wanted to see you again. She should return home soon. Can you not wait?"

Afra looked at his boots and bit his lip. He did not want to wait for Orna, ever. She looked good enough, with long blond hair and a slender figure, but she had little humor. He could never tease her as he teased Egyptus. He hoped he would never want to wait for her. "I am sorry, Auntie Amina, but my mama is waiting for these berries. I cannot wait any longer for her."

Amina sighed. "If you must leave, I suspect you should go quickly. Be careful not to spill the berries."

"Yes, Auntie," Afra said, moving toward the path that would take him home. "I will be careful." He hurried down the path until he turned a corner before stopping. It would do no good for him to spill the berries, and Auntie Amina had put them in an open basket.

He fished in the pocket he wore across his shoulder until he found his square of linen. It was not as clean as it had been that morning, but it was big enough to cover the basket. He tucked the cloth in along the edges.

He could not run. The berries would break free if he did. But he could jog down the path toward home. The sun had dropped to only a span above the western mountain. Mama would serve the evening meal soon, and he still had to cross more than half the valley.

I hope she knows I hurried as fast as I could. I do not want her to refuse to feed me again. Maybe Egyptus would take pity on me and feed me? What would she feed me? She makes an excellent stew and her flatbread is as good as Mama's. No. She is a friend, not someone I can go to when Mama refuses to feed me.

He pulled the basket close to his chest and sprinted toward home.

The paths emptied as he ran. Many families ate dinner when the sun neared the mountain. Most women had left something cooking when they left to meet with Grandmama so there would be a delicious dinner for their families. Afra could smell the aroma of food drifting through the open doors as he rushed past them.

His mouth watered. Someone had cherries cooking. He loved cherries. As he ran, he smelled roasts, soups, stews, and other good foods.

Mama, please remember you sent me off to the other side of the valley today.

He slid to a stop close to the path that led to his home. He glanced down at the basket of berries. Somehow, the cloth had stayed tucked around them, and they had not spilled.

Afra sucked in a big breath, ran his hand through his hair, strolled up the walk, and entered the home he had lived in since his birth.

Perhaps one day soon I will enter a home of my own with Egyptus. That will be nice. She will not deny me dinner if I am late.

"What do you think, Mama?" Abigayil asked. "How long can we continue as daughters of God?"

Egyptus twisted her head sharply toward her sister and mama. "What do you mean, Abigayil? Are we not all daughters of Jehovah?"

"Names are important," Abigayil said. They walked back along the path toward their home across the plain.

When the people left the small valley they had settled in shortly after the ark came to a rest and the earth dried, they had come here to the plains of Shinar where there was room for all the children and grandchildren.

Egyptus gazed out at the land belonging to her papa, Ham. He had received good, fertile land with a stream running from the hills across to the other side. It lay fallow now they had harvested the last of the grains. It rested during the cold of the year. This land fed them and the animals they raised.

"What does Shinar mean?" Ruth asked. "It must mean something."

"I never heard," Mama said.

"I know your name means Daughter of God," Abigayil said. "Why did your parents give you that name?"

"My mama and papa served Jehovah and wanted me to remember their love for Him," Mama said. "People have teased me much of my life because of my name. I do not mind. It helps me remember my mama and papa as much as I remember Jehovah."

"Why did you not give one of us your name?" Leah asked. "Are we not all daughters of God?"

"My earliest ancestors, after Eve and Adam, were Rebecca and Enos. Evil men stole two of their children and took them as prisoners to Nod as slaves. You do not know the wickedness of the city and land of Nod," Mama said.

"It was a city. Jehovah tells us not to concentrate in cities. Why?" Ruth asked, kicking a stone as she walked along the path.

"Nod was worse than most. People forget they are His children when they crowd into tightly packed homes. There is something about cities that invites the Destroyer into your lives. Avoid them if you can. My grandpapa and grandmama were those two children."

"Rebecca must have been sad when they took her children," Dodi said, patting the back of her youngest child as she carried her down the path. "Did they ever come back?"

"Ziva and Nat never saw their parents again," Mama said. "They married children of Nod."

"So you are a daughter of ... of —"

"Yes. A child of Cain. I carry the blood of Cain. I brought it through the flood so his family would live in us."

"I wondered if it was you," Egyptus said, linking her elbow with her mama's.

"My family served and worshiped Jehovah, but yes, we also carried the blood of Cain."

"Grandmama said the curse only affects those who listen to the Destroyer. You never have, Mama," Abigayil said.

"No, dear. I never have. I am careful to always worship Jehovah. We pray every day for you and our other children. We must be extra careful to avoid losing the blessings of Jehovah."

"What do we do if our children choose to disobey?" Egyptus asked.

"Does this mean you have someone you want to be the papa of your children?" Leah teased.

"No one has asked me yet," Egyptus answered. "But I hope he asks me soon." She let go of her mama's elbow and walked away from the others.

"I know who it is," Ruth sang in a singsong voice.

"You only think you know," Egyptus growled, although she smiled.

She had not allowed herself to think about which man she wanted to marry until recently. But she knew who she wanted to be the papa of her children, Afra.

"What do we do if our children disobey?" Mama brought her thoughts back to the question she had asked. Mama linked arms with Egyptus once more. "We pray. We love them. And we cry a lot."

"You do not keep them inside or force them to attend Sabbath services?" Ruth asked.

"Have I ever forced you to do something?" Mama asked. "Except to eat your vegetables and do what is necessary to stay safe? No. Even when you were little, I could not force you to do anything."

Egyptus saw Afra jogging toward them. *Will he stop to talk with me?*

She moved away from the others a bit as he hurried past.

Ruth grinned. "I like a challenge."

"Stubborn," Egyptus said with a little laugh.

"Afra?" Ruth teased.

"No, not Afra, you," Egyptus said in a louder voice so Ruth could hear.

He kept running, not even turning to see what she said. Maybe he was not the one. But why did her heart always race when she saw him?

Egyptus did not hear the things her mama and sisters said as she walked beside them, absorbed in her thoughts.

"Mama?" Leah asked as they turned up the path to Mama's home. "What did you do when your children and grandchildren left the faith?"

Egyptus jerked out of her thoughts to listen.

"I spent many nights watering my pillow with my tears. I tried to reason with them. I tried to teach them they could only find safety inside the faith. But they could not find wives and husbands inside, not the last of them." Mama sucked in a deep breath. "Dekar continued to trust Jehovah, but he could see no way forward. All the women, even all Shem's and Japheth's daughters, had deserted their faith in Jehovah for the idol gods. He had no hope for a wife and family. How could I insist he stay with us?" Tears leaked from Mama's eyes.

"My question remains unanswered," Abigayil said. "How long can we continue as daughters of God?"

"Until our death?" Leah asked.

"Until someone invites the Destroyer into her life?" Dodi asked.

"As long as we trust Jehovah," Mama said, stopping outside her door. "It is that simple. I have endured much in my life. Nothing has convinced me this trust is not precious. Not running from giants or wading through floods. Not even those days when others thought they could not trust me because of my mark. I know Jehovah loves me. I will never allow the Destroyer to change that."

"Family did not trust you?" Ruth squealed.

"Before they knew me, they did not. All they knew of me then was my mark. It peeked above my neckline then," Mama answered.

"I have not seen a mark on you," Abigayil said.

"Because it is no longer there. I have proved my faith and trust in Jehovah. He removed my mark."

"What brought you to meet Papa?" Ruth asked.

"You heard that story before," Dodi interrupted. "But why would Jehovah bring you to Papa?"

"I spent many years wondering that. I am nothing special. I believe my grandparents from long ago, Ziva and Nat, were taken to Nod for me. I have the blood of Cain and the blood of Enos and Adam in me. Jehovah promised Cain his posterity would not all be lost. I am the one who brought it through the flood into this new world." Mama rubbed her nose. "Do I smell something burning?"

Ruth flinched. "My dinner!" she rushed into the house.

Abigayil, Leah, and Dodi gathered their children to them. "We have our dinners to finish as well. Our husbands will expect food soon."

Within a few breaths, they kissed Mama goodbye and were gone. Mama turned to Egyptus as they entered the house. "Do you think Afra will talk to your papa soon?" she asked.

"Mama!" Egyptus cried, cringing. She followed her into the house. "I do not know. He acts like he cares for me, but ..." She lifted her shoulder in a small shrug. "I do not know if he will ask me to be his wife. Perhaps he is afraid of Papa?"

"Your papa is a loving grandpapa. Afra knows that."

"And he is my papa. Will that be a problem?"

Mama shook her head. "It should not be. You need a man to settle you down. Should I speak to Elva?"

"No, Mama!" Egyptus gasped. "If he cares for me, he will find his courage and ask me or Papa."

Proposal

"Tomorrow is wash day," Afra's mama announced at the end of the meal. "We will need many buckets of water heated if we are to get all your clothing clean. You girls need to bring water in tonight."

The girls grumbled as they gathered their water urns. "The boys could help," Lili said.

"We could, but we worked hard all day preparing for the threshing while you were off visiting with Grandmama Imma," Jeb said.

"We get one day away from so much work," Lili said.

"Your time away from work is ended," Mama said. "With the rain, we have more muddy clothing than usual to wash tomorrow."

Afra's sisters slumped out of the house with their water urns. One urn each would never fill the washtub.

If Mama is doing laundry and sending her girls for water, the other women will get water as well. Perhaps Egyptus will get water for her mama. I can help her. While there, perhaps I can ask her to marry me. Afra pulled his cloak on.

"I am going for a walk," he said to his mama.

As he neared the well, he grinned when he saw Egyptus carrying her urn. He reached out for it. "Do you need help?"

"Why would I need help? Just because I must carry many urns full of water to help wash clothing tomorrow?" Egyptus growled.

Afra sucked in a breath and bit his lip. "You need a well in your yard," he said.

"That would be nice, but ..."

"I know. You need water flowing close to the house to dig a well."

"Papa says no water flows beneath us."

"I have a plot of land I am building a house on. I plan to dig a well behind it."

"Do you plan to live alone? Or do you have someone in mind to share your house with you?" Egyptus asked, her voice softening.

He took her urn, set it beside the well, and dropped the bucket to the bottom. Pulling on the rope, he brought the bucket filled with water up and pulled it into Egyptus's urn. He dropped the bucket into the well again to fill the urn to the top.

Before Egyptus could pick it up, Afra lifted the urn to his shoulder and turned to carry it to her house. She walked beside him.

They walked in silence almost half the way to her home before he sucked in a breath and spoke. "Actually, ... erm ... I do have someone I want to share my home with. Would ... uh ... you consider ... uh..."

Stop stuttering and say it!

He worked to swallow the lump in his throat. "Will you be my wife?"

Egyptus stopped suddenly. Afra took two more steps before turning to stare at her. The water in the urn sloshed out and splashed on his tunic. Some splashed on her.

"Oh. It is cold. And you want me as your wife?" she asked, her eyes wide and her face stiff. "I thought you wanted one of Japheth's daughters or granddaughters. They hang around you all the time. And they are beautiful. I am not beautiful like them."

"Not beautiful?" Afra asked. He set the urn on the ground between them. "You are more beautiful than any of the other girls. And who else loves to milk cows early in the morning?"

"You want me to be your wife so I can milk your cows? I will not be your slave." She picked up the urn and marched toward her home.

"No! Egyptus!" Afra called and ran to catch up to her. "Let me carry that."

"I have carried two others this evening and will carry more. Why would you carry my urn? So you can splash the more of the water out?"

"You stopped so suddenly I could not help that some of the water splashed," Afra said.

"So now it is my fault you splashed?" She kept marching toward her home.

"Why are so unhappy with me?" Afra asked, running his hands through his hair."I thought you would be happy to become my wife."

They reached the path to her house. She stopped and stared at him. "Your wife, maybe. Not your milk maid and slave." Egyptus stomped with the urn to the back of the house and poured the water into the big pot they used for washing clothing.

Afra stood where she had left him, staring. *I thought she would be happy.*

Ruth sat beside the pot, stoking the fire so they would have hot water early the next morning.

"Trouble?" Afra heard Ruth say.

"No." Egyptus turned and pounded back toward the well with her urn in her arms.

"Egyptus," Afra said, hurrying to catch up to her. "I think I said something wrong."

She refused to look at him. "Did you?" Gripping the urn, she continued to tramp toward the well.

"Your love for my cows is only one reason I love you." His heart fluttered as he said it. It was true. He loved her.

"So we are back to the cows, are we?" Egyptus said between clenched teeth. "Do I look like a cow to you?" She set the urn beside the well and dropped the bucket in.

"You are the most beautiful woman on the plain of Shinar, on all the earth. You are fierce and gentle, tough and kind, hardworking and I feel peace when I am with you." He set his hands on hers and helped to pull the bucket back up.

He felt her twitch, but she did not shove his hands away. Her face was filled with contemplation.

"Egyptus, I am doing this all wrong. I love you." He grabbed the bucket and poured the water into the urn before dropping it back into the well. "I want to be here to help you draw your water. I want to be the one to watch our food grow together. I want to run my hands through your hair ..."

He lifted his hands from the rope and the bucket splashed down the well. He shook his head and grabbed the rope and and pulled it back up. "I want to be with you always. I want to sleep with you beside me and wake in the morning to find you still there."

Her face softened. "You would have to wake early to find me still in your bed."

Afra cleared his throat. The bucket reached the rim of the well. He grabbed it and poured the water into her urn. "I get up as early as you. It is my privilege to milk the cows each morning, and they do not like to wait."

He bent to lift her urn. "And Egyptus, I will dig a well for you so you do not have to carry heavy urns of water."

"What if I want to carry water? This is where my friends and I meet."

Afra glanced around. "I see no other friends here. Only me. Your friend, Afra."

"And you are my best friend," Egyptus said with a grin.

He walked toward her home. She walked beside him. "Will you marry me?"

"I do not know."

"Why?"

"Papa must give us permission."

"Oh." He carried the urn almost to her house, his thoughts churning. Could he speak to Grandpapa Ham, Egyptus's papa, about marrying his youngest daughter?

"Grandpapa Ham has always been loving and kind to me. If he agrees, will you marry me?"

Egyptus took the urn from his arms and smiled. "If Papa agrees, then, yes. I will marry you."

Afra leaned across the urn and kissed her gently on the cheek. "I will ask him tonight. Will that be soon enough?"

"You will not be the first." She quirked an eyebrow up. "If you can find him." She glanced at the stars that sparkled in the early evening sky.

"I know where he is. He and Papa are in the barn, examining the wheat."

"It will soon dry enough to thresh. It will keep us busy when it dries."

He grinned. "Yes, but we can work together."

"You do the threshing, you and the oxen. I will join the women lifting the wheat so the wind can blow away the chaff."

He brushed a lock of her hair back, happy to be with her. "I will find Grandpapa and ask him."

Egyptus hugged her urn to her body. "Will your mama and papa accept me as your wife?" Egyptus asked, her voice becoming small.

"We can ask them after I speak to Grandpapa." He kissed her cheek again and hurried toward the barn. His step carried a bounce.

Although her heart sang, Egyptus did not want to show her excitement to others. This was special and personal. She poured the water from the urn into the big wash pot and went inside to sit near her mama. The room had darkened.

Mama nodded toward the candles. "You will need a candle." She poked her needle through the seam in one of Papa's tunics.

Egyptus sucked in a deep breath and let it out slowly and quietly. Always mending.

She retrieved a candle from a table by the wall, then lit it off her mama's candle. She set it on the table beside her chair and reached into the mending basket.

"Has Papa returned from the wheat barn yet?" she asked.

Mama hummed. "Was he going to the wheat barn? All I know is he went to speak to our sons. He has much to do before the weather becomes too cold to work outside."

"Yes, Mama. But we already threshed the flax."

"And we still have wheat to thresh and winnow."

"Threshing is hard work."

Mama's lips lifted in a small smile. "All our work is difficult."

The women worked together, silently stabbing needles through the fabric.

"Will you want to tend the wash fire during the night or early in the morning so we can begin to wash early?" Mama asked.

"I filled the pot —"

"Which is your assignment."

"I will rise early and have the water hot and ready when you and Ruth rise from your rest." Egyptus grinned at her mama. You know I rise early."

"No milking for you tomorrow. We will have to wait for Canaan's sons to bring us milk."

"But I —" *I want to see Afra again and soon. I want him to kiss me once more, or many times.*

"You will not have time. You will be busy keeping the fire burning and the water hot enough for us to wash our clothing tomorrow. Be certain to gather all your dirty clothing tonight."

"I know, Mama. And bring my bedding when I go out to tend the wash water."

Mama nodded. "You have done this before."

"And I will do it again and again, every month until I die."

"And I will continue to do so until I am too bent and broken to wash our clothing. Then I will call on you or another daughter or granddaughter to wash your papa's and my dirty clothing."

"I will be happy to wash yours and Papa's clothing," Egyptus said.

After many long breaths with only the sound of their needles poking through the fabric of the clothing they mended breaking the silence, Mama spoke again. "Why were you looking for your papa?"

"I did not look for him."

"He should return soon. You asked about him. Why?"

"Nothing." Egyptus licked her lips. *I should not have said anything. Now she will want to know.*

"Nothing?" Mama glanced up.

Egyptus lifted a shoulder. "Afra said he would find him."

"And how does Afra seeking your papa affect you?"

"Maybe not at all. Maybe a lot."

Mama dropped her mending into her lap and stared into her daughter's eyes. "Egyptus?"

Egyptus tied a knot and bit the thread off, trying to think how best to answer. "Afra is building a home."

Mama's gaze did not move from her eyes. "And?"

"And he needs a wife for his home."

Mama continued to stare. "And?"

"And he asked me to be that wife. He asked me to marry him." Egyptus bit her lip and picked a hair off her skirt.

"And you said yes?"

"I did, if Papa allows it."

"You have waited for this for many months."

Egyptus grinned. "Many years."

Mama tipped her head back and allowed her rich laugh to fill the room. "We have wondered how long it would take Afra to ask you," she said when she could speak again.

"We? We, who?"

"Me. Papa. Elva. Canaan."

Egyptus tipped her head to the side. "Why?"

Mama put a hand over her mouth and giggled some more.

"Mama!" Egyptus tried to ignore her mama's glee, stabbing her needle through the seam.

Mama sucked in her breath and held it until she stopped laughing. "We have watched the two of you since you were little. You followed Afra around since you could walk. He slowed to wait for you. We have seen a love between you for longer than I can say."

Egyptus swallowed and folded the dress she completed. "You have seen for that long? Why did you insist I stop helping him milk in the morning?"

"To give him a gentle nudge. We wondered how long it would take for him to miss you there beside him. We did not expect it to take only one day."

"Perhaps he planned to ask me to marry him all along?"

"He may have, but he took his time."

"Perhaps he wanted to have a home for us first."

"He should want that. However, he could declare his love and ask you to marry him before he built it." Mama picked up her mending and stabbed her needle through the seam.

Egyptus set the mended dress aside and dug through the basket for something else to mend.

"You should take the one on top," Mama suggested.

"Why? Those on bottom have waited longer."

"After you stir them around, it does not matter," Mama agreed.

Egyptus took the top item and searched for the seam that needed mending. When she found it, she tied a knot in her thread and stuck her needle through.

She and Mama worked together, saying nothing of importance, until Papa opened the door. He slipped his boots off and left them inside the door before coming to sit with them.

"Where is Ruth?" he asked.

"Outside tending the fire. Tomorrow is wash day. If we are to have hot water, we must keep the fire burning through the night," Mama replied.

Papa sighed. "Someday that will not be necessary."

Egyptus jerked her head up and stared at her papa. "How will that happen?"

"Papa says he has seen water coming from a ... round thing into a bowl in the cooking space. He has seen the future until the end."

"Hot water without heating it over a fire? It would be wonderful," Egyptus said with a sigh.

"Do not get your hopes up," Papa warned. "It is in the future. Far in the future. You will carry water and heat it all your life."

She sighed, but deeper than Papa. "It would be nice if it happened now."

Papa sat and watched them work, massaging the back of Mama's neck. At last he spoke. "I had a visitor a while ago."

Egyptus stopped sewing and stared at her papa. "Oh?"

"Afra came to ask if I would agree to a marriage between him and you."

She sucked in a breath and stared into her papa's face, trying to discern the answer. Papa had learned long ago to keep the answers hidden. "What did you tell him?"

"No."

Answer

A fra walked toward the wheat barn, searching for his papa and grandpapa.

How am I to ask him? Should I throw myself at his feet?

He took a few more steps.

No. Be the man he would want for his daughter. Ask him without flourish.

Inside the barn, he saw his papa and all the uncles with his grandpapa, standing in a loose circle, discussing something. Afra turned to walk away when his papa saw him.

"Afra. We need you to go through the wheat and determine if it is dry enough to thresh tomorrow."

Would it be dry this fast? We only cut it yesterday.

"Yes, Papa. You remember the women plan to wash clothing tomorrow?"

"No. I did not. You still need to go through the wheat. If it is almost ready, we can plan to thresh the day after the Sabbath."

Afra fought the slump threatening to drag his shoulders down. *I do not mind the work of threshing the wheat, but I have to talk with Grandpapa. Why is Papa making it so difficult?* He threw them back and walked to the first sheaf of wheat, touching it. The wheat on the edge had dried significantly, but not enough to thresh. Perhaps two, maybe three more days.

He walked between the sheaves, running his hands through the wheat. Some fell to the floor, but not enough to consider threshing soon.

When he reached the other side, Grandpapa Ham stood there watching. "Is it dry enough yet?"

"Not yet. Some falls to the floor, but most still cling to the stalks. It may be dry enough after the Sabbath."

Grandpapa nodded. "I did not expect it to be dry enough yet. Your papa and uncles thought it would be, since it is drying in the barn rather than in the fields. It gets more air outside."

"I thought the same thing, Grandpapa," Afra said. He swallowed. Alone with Grandpapa for the first time in many days. He had to ask.

As Grandpapa Ham turned away, Afra touched his arm. "Grandpapa? I have something I need to ask you."

Grandpapa turned to face him with clenched teeth. "Well, boy, ask."

Afra sucked in a deep breath and let the words tumble out. "Egyptus and I have been friends as long as I can remember, since she was big enough to follow me. We love each other. I am building a home for us on the edge of the valley. Will you give us your permission to marry?"

Grandpapa Ham rolled in his lips and stared at Afra for many long breaths. Then, his shaggy white head moved back and forth. "No, son. I cannot allow you to marry my Egyptus."

He grimaced. "I know you and Egyptus have been close. It will break her heart when I tell her. We have waited for you to have the courage to ask. I told no one how I planned to answer. It will make your mama and Basya as sad as it will make Egyptus. But I must still tell you no."

Afra bit his lower lip as unexpected tears fought to fall. "Will you tell me why? Is there something I can change in myself that will change your mind?"

"I will tell you, but I doubt you can change my mind. Jehovah cursed your papa, Canaan, before we left our first home here in this new world. He and his sons are not allowed to use or receive the Priesthood of Jehovah."

"I cannot change the curse brought on me and my brothers by my papa." Afra bowed his head, staring at his boots. "I love your daughter. She loves me."

"I know. It hurts me to tell you no, for I know you will be good to her, better than some of the other men who have asked me for her. However, I want Egyptus to marry one who can receive those blessings."

"I understand," Afra said, no longer fighting back his tears. "I would want it for my daughter as well. I will always love Egyptus."

"And she will always love you."

Grandpapa waited near, not offering comfort for many long breaths, as though considering Afra's words.

"Afra," he said at last. "No man will love my daughter as you do and she will love no man as she loves you. I know if I continue to say no, she will accept my will, as you have."

Afra rubbed at his chest, trying to relieve the tension there. There was no other woman for him.

"For that reason," Grandpapa Ham continued, "I will change my answer. It would not be fair to another man to have you always there in Egyptus's heart."

Afra lifted his gaze to his grandpapa's face, his mind slow to understand his grandpapa's meaning. "Then, you will —"

"Yes. I will allow you to marry my last daughter. I know you will be good to her. You will love and bless her."

"I will. Thank you, Grandpapa!" Afra flung his arms around his grandpapa briefly, then rushed away, leaping and shouting for joy.

Grandpapa had given him permission! When should he go tell Egyptus?

He saw Grandpapa walk toward his home, enter, and close the door behind him.

Not now. I will tell her in the morning.

Egyptus rose earlier than usual. She had spent the night dreaming of Afra after Papa had shared his reasoning and change of mind. She gathered her clothing and bedding into a huge basket. She carried it out through the cooking area to the back of the house. There she found Mama tending the fire.

"Oh, hello Egyptus," Mama said. "You are here early."

"Sleep evaded me. I slept a while, then woke with thoughts of Afra and what I would need for our home. I decided I could tend the fire and allow you to get some rest."

Mama yawned and touched Egyptus's shoulder. "Thank you. I am getting older. This is harder than it used to be."

"We all are, Mama," Egyptus laughed.

"You will feel it differently when you are my age," Mama said with a wave as she staggered into the house.

Egyptus emptied her basket and sorted the clothing into piles. No need to ruin her light-colored clothing with the dye that ran from the darker clothing.

Faint light shone over the eastern mountain when she rubbed soap into the hot water. She stirred it in and her face, hands, and arms heated from the steam. Hot. Very. It would clean her clothing.

Mama is tired. I will surprise her.

Egyptus slipped quietly through the house and picked up Mama's basket of dirty clothing. She carried it out and dumped it with hers, sorting it into piles that would fit into the washtub.

She lifted the clothing into the pot with her long wooden paddle and stirred them. She poured cool water from the nearby urn into a smaller pot, then added hot water. Into this, she dropped some clothing from the tub.

She scrubbed each item of clothing, looking for spots of dirt, then scrubbed each one some more before dipping it into a pot of cool, clean water.

After rinsing all the soap from the clothing, she hung them over the lines Papa had strung between trees the night before.

As she dipped more clothing into the pot of warm water, Afra strode around the corner of the house.

"You are up early," he said.

With tousled hair and wrinkled clothing, he looked like he had slept no better than her. "When am I not up early?"

He chuckled. "If you are not up early, I fear you are ill."

Egyptus giggled. "And I am rarely ill."

"I hoped to find you here this morning. I wanted to talk to you last night, but I saw your papa enter the house and did not see him leave."

"He strung these lines last night," Egyptus said, nodding to the lines between the trees.

"I did not see him." Afra stepped close. "Your papa told me no."

"I heard."

"But then, he reconsidered and gave us permission to marry."

"I heard that too. I thought you would come tell me last night."

Egyptus grinned. "I know. Papa can be frightful sometimes."

Afra ducked his head. "He can. But he gave us permission."

Egyptus turned from her pot of washing. "Yes. When will you complete your, I mean, our home?"

"It depends on how much time it will take to thresh and winnow the wheat. If I get some help from my brothers, I will finish it in two or three weeks."

Egyptus threw her arms around him. The warm, earthy smell coming from him filled warmed her. He was hers. "That is wonderful!" Then, she remembered all she needed to do. "And so fast. I hope I can get everything I need finished in time."

"What do you have to do?"

Egyptus returned to the washing, pushing the clothing under the water once more. "I need a big tub for washing, plus smaller pots and urns. I will need pots for cooking. Bedding." A thrill ran down her back. *We will sleep together!* She shook it off and rubbed clothes up and down with each item she mentioned. "Cooking and eating utensils, plates, cups, a rug for our floors to keep our feet warm, and so many more things I have not even thought of yet."

"I thought you had some of those things made," Afra said, gently pulling her hands from the hot water and putting them around his neck. "Your sisters and the other women of the family will help."

"I know, but there is so much to prepare, especially when I look at my mama's home."

Afra kissed her cheek. It felt good to allow him this affection. "Your mama has had many years to provide all the things she has in her home. I am certain she had much less when she and Grandpapa walked off the ark."

"Yes," Egyptus said, allowing water to drip down Afra's neck.

He did not flinch. Instead, he pulled her closer and kissed her on the mouth. *Our first kiss, and we will have many more of these.*

"We can live with much less as well. We can make what you do not have," he said.

"You will be happy with that?" Egyptus leaned back in his arms to stare into his eyes.

"Yes. I will be happy to have you and blankets to wrap around us to keep away the cold."

"We will have more than that. And you should remember to make us a bed." She slipped from his arms and dunked her hands into the warm water.

"I have already started work on our bed. I would not forget something so important." He kissed her behind the ear, sending shivers along her body. "I must go milk the cows. They are waiting for me."

"I would like to go with you ..."

"But you have the washing to do. The cows will still give us milk even if my brothers and my rough hands milk them."

He strode away. She spun around and watched him leave, holding a dripping tunic in her hands.

Two or three weeks. How soon will Grandpapa Noah be willing to marry us? Ruth plans to marry Hayam soon. Will it be before Afra finishes our home?

As she pondered all the questions racing through her head, she washed and rinsed most of hers and her mama's clothing before Ruth came yawning through the door.

"You have been busy," Ruth said.

"I rose early. There is room in the tub for your light-colored clothing. I will finish the last of mine and Mama's while you sort yours."

Later, Mama opened the back door, rubbing her eyes. "Someone took my clothing."

"I came for it while you slept. I started early, since the water was hot and I was awake," Egyptus said.

Mama blinked, then smiled. "Thank you, darling. What will I do when you two live in your own home?"

"Do your own washing?" Egyptus asked with a giggle.

"Probably," Mama said.

"What do you mean when Egyptus lives in her own home?" Ruth asked.

"Afra talked to Papa last night. He asked me to marry him."

"He did? At last?" Ruth squealed. "When?"

"We have not set a date yet. He still must complete our home."

"I saw him working on a home on the west edge of the valley," Ruth said. "Is that the one?"

"I do not know," Egyptus admitted. "He has not shown me the house. He only told me he wanted to share it with me, and that he will dig a well for me."

"I will," Afra said coming around the corner of the house with a bucket of milk. "Where do you want me to pour this? Egyptus used to bring your milk. She did not come to help this morning."

Mama grinned and waved to the blue urn by the back door. "Pour milk into the blue urn we always use. It is the one Egyptus brought with her."

Afra chuckled. "I should have known." He poured the milk into the urn. "Would you like me to show you our house later?"

"I would," Egyptus cried. Excitement filled her. *Lovely words, our house. I did not expect to hear those words from him.*

"You two need to speak with Grandpapa Noah soon," Mama suggested.

"I will be back for you to go speak with him in —" He glanced up at the sun. "A little more than a span. I must help deliver the rest of this milk and then eat."

"We need to eat as well," Mama said.

Afra bent and kissed Egyptus on the cheek. "Until then," he whispered and strode around the house.

"I know you have been busy with the laundry, Egyptus, but did you think of a morning meal? It is still your responsibility."

Egyptus glanced at the clothing hanging across the lines as her face burned. "No, Mama. I did not. I forgot it was now my responsibility. I will go start it now."

She ran into the kitchen and found flat bread in a bowl, wrapped in a cloth. *Mama, you tease me.*

Surprises

The women were cleaning up after the washing when Afra returned from delivering the milk and eating. "Are we ready to go see Grandpapa Noah?" he asked.

He took Egyptus's hand and walked with her across the plain to Grandpapa Noah's home.

"We cannot see much of each other after today," Afra said as they walked.

"Why not?"

"I will be spending my time finishing our home. I have finished some, but much work is still required."

"I understand. I have much to do to prepare as well," Egyptus said.

"You will have some time."

Afra pulled her close as they walked together.

Grandpapa Noah greeted the young couple and led the way inside when they spoke of needing a favor. "Your grandmama is out with some other women washing clothing," he said, waving toward the back of the house.

He offered them a cool drink of water, then sat in a chair across from them. "What can I help you two with this beautiful day?"

Afra glanced at Egyptus before turning to face Grandpapa Noah. "Will you join us in marriage when I finish building our home?"

Grandpapa's face glowed. "This is good news. I love to marry young couples. I have watched you two for many years and wondered when you would decide to marry."

"Was it that obvious to everyone?" Egyptus asked, crimson rising above the neck of her dress. "Mama says they have waited as well. I did not expect it."

Afra grinned and shuffled his feet on the floor. "I have loved Egyptus for a long time. I did not know if her papa would accept me, or if she would. Grandpapa Ham is a kind man, but he is my grandpapa and Egyptus's papa."

"And?" Grandpapa Noah questioned. "How would that be a problem?"

Afra rubbed the back of his neck. "I did not know if he would accept me, as Canaan's son. The curse ... And Egyptus is Papa's brother."

"The curse could have been a problem. I cannot change it. However, when the children of Adam and Eve married, all they had to choose from to marry were brothers and sisters, and later the children of brothers and sisters for many years. Since we, like Adam and Eve, are in a new world, with no one to marry except brothers and sisters and the children of brothers and sisters or aunts or uncles, who else would you marry?"

"I had not thought about it that way," Egyptus said. "I suppose marriage is easier for us. We have the children and grandchildren of three couples to choose from, not just our own brothers and sisters."

"You would choose a man from another family?" Afra asked. *Would you accept any of the others? Your papa said you would not.*

"Why would I? I love you and you love me."

He wiped his forehead with the back of his hand in relief.

Grandpapa Noah laughed. "You two are good for each other. I have seen it since you were little. When do you plan to marry?"

"When I complete my, er," Afra glanced at Egyptus, "our home. I need a place for us to live."

"You do not want to live with your mama and papa?" Grandpapa asked.

"No!" Afra yelped.

Grandpapa grinned. "Few men willingly choose to take their new wife into the home of his parents. It is better that he does not. Your wife deserves her own home and the responsibility of caring for it without a mama criticizing everything she does."

"Few women want to move into a home to be criticized," Egyptus said. "Not that Elva would criticize me. Although, she and Mama do things differently. It would be difficult to fit in. It is hard enough to do things the way Mama insists when I can see a better way. Besides," Egyptus glanced at Afra. "There are lots more men in that home now than mine. It could be ... difficult."

Grandpapa smirked. "You will want a home of your own. How much have you completed?"

"I have worked to help the others of our family with harvesting and threshing the grains during the last of this warm season," Afra replied. "Even so, I have the walls up and the roof is on. I have stones gathered from the fields to build a fire space, maybe two. It is a good beginning."

"Is it a problem for Afra to show me our new home before we marry? Some seem to think that is a problem."

Grandpapa leaned back in his chair and ran his hand through his beard. "Some follow old customs for no reason. We follow most because they help us stay close to Jehovah. We work six days and rest and worship Him on the Seventh Day. We bow down to no other idols or gods, remembering Jehovah blesses and protects us. We take great care in the ways we speak of Jehovah and Father, not using their names to make simple oaths or using them without thought."

"We love our God and honor him," Afra said.

Grandpapa Noah shifted in his chair. "We seek to be honest in all we do, especially in our love for our wives and children, taking no other women as concubines or second wives. We honor our parents in love. We honor life and do not kill, except when we need meat. We do not steal. We speak the truth and work for our food and homes, not taking nor hoping for that which our brother has."

Afra shifted in his chair. *Those are all good commandments we obey, but what about the customs? Must I wait to show Egyptus our home until after we marry?*

"All those are important to remember," Egyptus agreed. "We work together as families, not fighting among ourselves, most of the time."

"That is true," Grandpapa Noah said. "But the customs and ways of doing things are not all that important. Continue to build your home and your papa will approve it to ensure you do not take your new wife into an uncomfortable and unsafe home. In the ancient days, when Adam and his children built homes, they needed their wives to help build them. In this new land, our wives have helped build our homes as well."

"Mama helped build our home?" Egyptus asked, her eyes popping open. She and Papa had married many years before they built their home here. "Can I help Afra with our home?"

"I see no reason why you should not, if you have the time."

Afra sat up straighter. "I have brothers and other male family members who will help me." He took Egyptus's hands in his. "I would rather not wear your hands to blisters carrying stones. But I would love to have you advise me."

"You are a wise man, Afra. The advice of a good woman, especially our wives, should always be welcome," Grandpapa Noah said.

"Can we come again and set a time for our marriage when I complete the house?" Afra asked.

"Of course. Until then, I hope to see you in our family gathering for the Sabbath in two weeks."

"We are gathering as a whole family, then?" Egyptus asked.

Grandpapa nodded. "We must meet. I have received word from Jehovah I must share. It is good to gather. The rain and snow will come soon, and it will not be possible to join as a family."

"Will you give us a hint of what Jehovah has said?" Egtyptus asked.

Grandpapa shook his head. "No. I will share it with everyone at the same time. But I expected you to ask. It would surprise me if you were incurious."

Egyptus nodded. "I am nothing if not curious."

"I noticed," Afra said.

Egyptus and Afra hurried from their grandpapa Noah's home toward the west where the sun would set in the evenings. "I want your opinion on some things in our home," he said.

A thrill zipped up her spine. "Where is this house of yours, the one that will be ours?" she asked.

"Near the edge of the plain, close to the mountain, away from the others. No one has claimed land out there and there is a pretty little meadow with a spring and trees. We will have a beautiful place to raise our children."

"Will there be room for cows?"

He laughed and kissed her. "Those cows belong to Papa, but he told me he would give me two as a wedding gift."

"Oh? You told him you asked me to marry you?" Egyptus bent her head to the side and smiled up at him.

"I did not need to tell them. Papa and Mama have known I would ask you for a long time. They just did not know when."

"As did my mama and papa. What will we do there in your ... our little home?"

"Besides milk cows, love each other, and teach our children to love Jehovah?"

Egyptus loved Afra's goofy little grin when he teased her. "Yes. Besides all that. We will need something to trade with others for food and other things. Your papa trades milk. Mine has fields of grain he shares and trades with the others in the family. Uncle Japheth tans cow hides and the hides of other animals you men have hunted. His sons make beautiful items from that leather."

Afra squeezed Egyptus's hand. "Yes. Uncle Shem gathers wood from the hills. His sons carve and build from it. I went to them for wood for our home."

"What will we do? What will we create to share with others? Have you considered this?" Egyptus persisted.

"Mama makes cheese for our family. We can begin with the milk from our cows and make cheese to trade."

Egyptus grinned. "That is a good start. We can find other things to trade for what we need."

"And you will grow a vegetable garden for us." Afra glanced down at her.

She frowned up at him, then giggled. "You know I will."

After walking almost a span, they arrived at the half-built home. Only the walls and roof had been completed. Afra showed Egyptus the inside and talked with her about his plans. She approved most and made suggestions for others.

"Grandpapa Noah is correct," Afra said. "A man should listen to the suggestions of his woman. Your ideas will make our home warmer and more comfortable."

"I will bring blankets, dishes, and other things to make it comfortable."

"I will ask Arphaxad and his sons to make us furniture. Papa will help me make our bed."

"I thought we would sleep on the floor, wrapped in blankets." Egyptus winked at him.

"No. I never ... You are teasing me." His scrunched up face softened and he laughed.

"Yes, I am. We will have a wonderful home." Egyptus stared up at the roof. "I see no sparkles of light. The roof looks tight."

"No rain came through in the last storm. I have a good beginning. Now to complete it."

"We will be far from our parents' home."

Afra gazed toward the east and the milking barn. "I did not like the land closer to them. It is rocky. This land is more fertile. Come with me."

He led her out the back. Behind the home, fruit trees grew in orchard groves near the house. "We will have fruit to share with other families. We will have much to share and trade."

Egyptus threw her arms around Afra. "You were keeping this from me."

"I wanted to surprise you."

"You make me happy."

They walked under the trees and plucked the last of the pears and some apples growing in the small apple orchard.

"These will taste good with our dinner tonight," Egyptus said.

"*Our* dinner?" he asked.

"I will ask mama if I can invite you to join us. You are almost family."

Afra stopped short and set his fists on his hips. "I *am* family."

"Yes, but you are also part of Canaan's family. Mama will be happy to have you join us." She skipped ahead of him toward their new home. "And she will be happier with these pears to add to the meal."

Afra jogged to catch up with her. "Have I told you I love you?"

"Not in the last span."

"Egyptus, I love you." He put an arm around her waist and kissed her cheek.

She snuggled closer to his hip, enjoying his touch. "I love you as well, Afra. I look forward to our marriage and being together all the time. I want to make cheese with you and grow fruit to share."

"I will hurry to finish our home. I want to be with you all the time."

As they passed the barns, shouting erupted from within the wheat barn.

"What is going on in there?" Egyptus asked.

"The wheat must be nearly dry enough to thresh. It was close yesterday when I checked it," Afra said.

They peeked into the barn in time to see Canaan and Afra's brothers pounding on a small pile of wheat.

"We will thresh after the Sabbath," Afra told Egyptus.

"And then store the grains in the silos for next year."

"Then I will have time to finish our home."

"I will be called on to help with the stritching of the flax, preparing it to weave. I will need both the flax and wool to finish weaving blankets and fabric for a dress."

"Stritching is as difficult as threshing," Afra said. "We will be by your side, helping to soften the flax for weaving."

"We always have much work to do. Cool weather does not relieve us of work," Egyptus said with a sigh.

Afra kissed her before walking with her to her mama's house.

Mama stepped out the back door as they came around the corner. "Did you talk with Grandpapa Noah?" she asked.

"We did," Egyptus said. "He encouraged me to see my new house and make suggestions."

"And you did?" Mama asked.

"Yes, Mama. We went out there. Afra's ... our house is on the west edge of the plain."

"That is why I did not see you building it," Mama said, nodding to Afra. "Few people live out there."

"That is why I chose it. The land is rich and fruit trees grow there. We will have fruit to share with others," Afra said.

"All you need now is to finish your home," Mama said, gazing at Afra.

"And for me to gather and finish everything I need to furnish it," Egyptus said.

"I will help you, as will others from the family. As the men will help Afra, the women will help you, as they have helped Ruth. We will have two weddings soon," Mama said.

"It is good for us to help each other," Afra said. He gave Egyptus a quick kiss before striding away toward his papa's home.

She set her hand on her mouth where he kissed her, feeling the heat of his lips. *I want more of this. Our home will not be finished soon enough.*

"Are you ready for this?" Mama asked.

"Yes, Mama. I am."

Organizing

After a quiet Sabbath worshiping together in the field outside Grandpapa Ham's house, threshing the wheat took most of the next day. The women spread bundles of wheat on the smooth rock of the threshing floor and stepped back. The men then beat the wheat with the long flails Afra and his brothers had repaired, breaking the grain away from the chaff.

They stopped at intervals, allowing women to add more grain. When the grain piled too high for the flails to break down the staves of wheat, the men rested while the women filled baskets with broken staves, chaff, and grain. They set the baskets aside, then laid more wheat on the threshing floor.

As the process repeated through the day, Afra touched Egyptus's hand each time she passed. She turned and smiled at him, making a spot over his heart warm. It made him want to work harder to show her she had made a good choice.

At midday, everyone stopped to eat the cold meat, cheese, and bread the women had brought with them in baskets. Afra found Egyptus and sat with her, ignoring the teasing from the other young men.

"It is good you finally asked Egyptus to marry you," Jeb said. "I thought to ask her myself."

Afra grinned. "I win. We can be together more now whenever we want."

"Well, almost whenever we want," Egyptus teased. "You will be busy building our home while I will gather things to fill it. And we cannot spend the night together yet."

Afra covered his face with his hands and shook his head. "Oh, Egyptus." *I love how you tease me like I tease you.*

He could hear the giggling grin in her voice. "You said it."

"One day," he murmured. He removed his hands from his eyes to gaze into hers. "One day we can spend all our days and all our nights together."

"I look forward to that day." Egyptus blushed and slipped her hand into his.

His brothers and the other young men could tease him about this if they wanted. Afra dreamed of holding Egyptus in his arms all night.

Amor whistled as Afra kissed Egyptus on the cheek. "You wish you had a beautiful woman to kiss as well. What are you waiting for?" Afra asked.

"We have been waiting for you. Now we can look for a woman," Jeb said.

Afra's brothers lay back on the broken wheat staves where they sat and hooted.

All too soon, Grandpapa Ham signaled for everyone to clean up their meals. *Time to work again.*

Afra watched Egyptus put their uneaten food into her basket and set it with the others near the wall, then gather more sheaves of wheat to spread on the threshing floor. He longed to take her in his arms and kiss her deeply.

He picked up his flail and stood ready to beat the wheat from the chaff.

Later, when gathering the wheat and broken staves from the floor, Egyptus brushed up against Afra. "Are you rested yet?"

The touch of her body took his breath away. He gulped. *I must get our home finished.* "Not yet. It takes work to beat this wheat."

"Perhaps I will take my time filling the next basket."

Afra allowed the shock to show on his face, his eyes bulged. "No. Do not do that. Grandpapa will not be happy with you. By the time you women fill the baskets and empty the floor, I will be rested enough." He smiled. "Then you can sit and rest for a while."

"It seems unfair. You rest while I work, I rest while you work."

"But I can watch you work. It helps me." Afra grinned and waggled his eyebrows.

"Afra!" Egyptus cried, bumping him with her hip.

He giggled and watched her sway across the floor with the filled basket. *I can wait. But I must hurry with that house.* Desire filled him. They would soon have all the wheat threshed.

Before the sun set, they had flailed and gathered all the grain into baskets. It was ready for the next breezy day when they would winnow it. Even with this many people working, it would take another day to winnow all the wheat.

Afra took Egyptus's hand and walked from the wheat barn out into the late afternoon air. Now everyone knew they were to wed.

"You did not get anything done on our house today," Egyptus said.

"Food is more important. We must eat. I will be out there tomorrow, if we are not winnowing. When we get the wheat stored and ready for you women to cook, I will work there every day. I want us to move in and use some of this wheat."

Afra woke the next morning to a cool, breezy day. He sent Amor to tell Grandpapa Ham that it would be a good day to winnow even before they milked the cows.

Afra and his brothers quickly milked the cows and delivered the milk to the families, knowing they would all want to hurry to the winnowing. His mama had flat bread filled with cooked eggs and cheese for them to eat as they rushed toward the winnowing area.

Afra, Jeb, and Amor were among the last to arrive. Afra hastened to Egyptus's side. She welcomed him with a kiss on his cheek and handed him one of the forked tools he would use to throw the threshed wheat into the air. "Another day of work," he said.

"But I will not watch you today. I will work near you," she said.

"Too bad, I love to watch you work."

"And I love watching your muscles bulge."

Afra pointed at his arms. "These?"

"Yes," Egyptus said, grinning. "And those." She pointed to his legs.

They spent the day near each other, tossing the broken wheat staffs into the air. The lighter, broken staves, and other bits blew away, leaving only the wheat kernels to fall to the winnowing floor. Last, they used smaller, shallow baskets to shake the wheat into the air, allowing the last little bits of chaff to blow away in the breeze. They dumped the cleaned wheat into bigger baskets and later, into large lid-covered urns. Men carried the urns into the storage barn and placed them along the walls and out onto the floor, filling much of the barn.

At the end of the day, Afra plodded with Egyptus back to her home, happy that Mama Basya prepared a hot soup and invited him to join them for the evening meal.

"We will have farther to go next year," Afra said.

"Unless we spend a night here with Mama and Papa."

Afra frowned, unsure how he felt about that. But he and Egyptus would be together. That was all that mattered.

Over the next two weeks, Egyptus and Ruth went through all the things they had made and gathered earlier to take to their married homes.

Ruth frowned. "I thought I would marry and live with Haym long before you were even asked. I thought he would have completed our home by now. He had not taken me to see it yet, so I do not know how much more work is needed."

Perhaps you should whine less and show you are happy to be with him more.

While Ruth went through the blankets and rugs in her chest, Mama helped Egyptus pull dishes and pots from several hiding places that Egyptus had forgotten about. She had made some dishes many years ago, when she was young. Their quality was not as good as those she made later.

"You will remember the time you made these when you use them," Mama said as she set the dishes into a basket.

"Do you have any from when you were small?" Egyptus tucked smaller cups into the basket with the plates and bowls.

"You forget, Egyptus. I left everything I made as a young woman in my home, fleeing from giants and fire. I only have one thing from my childhood, Grandpapa Nat's journals." Mama set larger serving bowls in the basket with the other dishes.

"How sad for you, Mama."

"Grandmama and your aunties were generous with us, and your papa had a home from before we met. We used some pots, dishes, and bedding his first wife brought to her marriage." Mama set the basket aside and emptied another one onto the table to see what was in it. "Pots in this one."

"What happened to her, Mama?" Egyptus examined the pots she lifted from the basket.

"She and her child died in childbirth. Healers could not heal her illness. Not even Mama Imma could help her."

With the basket empty, they sorted through the pots, setting them back inside the basket Mama had set on the floor.

"Look at this one. You made it when you were eight," Mama said.

"How do you remember?" Egyptus shook her head. "I did not know mamas could die in childbirth. How sad for Papa, but good for you." She lifted out a smaller pot and set it into a larger one.

"Papa still mourned their deaths when I met him. Talk to him about it. It is his story to tell, not mine." Mama twisted and turned a pot in her hands, examining it for cracks. "This one will not hold water. It is broken." She set the pot aside to go into the midden heap. "Babies and mamas can die. We must be careful when the time comes for their birth."

"I want you to help with the births of my children," Egyptus said, examining her pots more carefully before putting them into the basket. "Have you lost any children?"

"Only before we entered the ark. Those women did not listen to my directions. Since we left the ark, between Grandmama Imma and me, we have lost no babies or mamas. I believe much of that is because Jehovah is blessing us. He knows we need every child to multiply and replenish this earth."

Three more pots had cracks, making them unusable and were set aside.

"We cannot multiply if our children do not live. Is that why we have fewer illnesses now? You tell stories of severe illnesses before," Egyptus asked, setting a pot in the basket.

"There were many illnesses then. We are on a clean land here. The flood washed away the diseases we suffered before, for now. Some will return when people forget Jehovah." Mama set the last pot in the basket. "You will want to make more pots before your wedding. You need large pots for heating water and an extra-large one for washing your bodies and clothing."

"Will I have time to make big pots before the rain and snow comes?"

Mama nodded and pushed the heavy basket away with her foot. "You should."

"Why would people forget Jehovah? He gives us everything, especially this beautiful earth."

ANGELIQUE CONGER

Mama sat with her hands on the table, tracing the lines in the wood. "It has happened already, some. Nimrod already leads some astray. It will get worse. You will see. The Destroyer will find a way, an opening to exploit. Because we live in an imperfect world, it will get worse."

Egyptus set her elbows on the table. "But we have lived all these years with no problems," she argued.

"Few problems, but we have had some. Some remember Cain and try to stay away from me because my fading mark 'taints' me."

"Grandmama says it is gone." Egyptus leaned forward. "I know Canaan lost the right to the priesthood. Will that follow me when I marry Afra? Will Jehovah still love us?"

"Jehovah will love you. I do not know about the other. That is for your papa and grandpapa to learn from Jehovah. Perhaps Grandpapa Noah will make some announcement next Sabbath when all the family gathers. We have not met often to worship, as the family has grown so large. I suspect there will be a sacrifice."

"Grandpapa has not sacrificed for some time. I look forward to it. I feel closer to Jehovah during a sacrifice."

"It helps us remember Him," Mama said, sitting up and stretching her back. "Do you have any other baskets here in the kitchen?"

"I think there is one more in the storage shed. I will get it."

"You will need help to carry it," Mama said. "Ruth, please come help."

In a few breaths, Ruth came into the kitchen. "How can I help, Mama?"

"Egyptus needs help to carry a basket from the storage shed. Please help her?"

Ruth glanced at her sister. "Yes. But I will need help with this blanket."

Do you think your needs are greater than mine? Will Hayam have your home ready before Afra has our finished.

"Gladly," Mama replied. "The house will be quiet with both of you girls married."

"Hayam says we will set a date when we see Grandpapa Noah next Sabbath," Ruth said.

"Two weddings so close together. And then my home will be empty again," Mama said, wetting her lips.

"Oh, Mama," the two young women cried, rushing to throw their arms around her.

"We will be close enough I can come visit every day," Ruth said.

"And I will come as often as I can," Egyptus added. "I will try to come on wash day."

Assistance

A fra gazed up, hoping no clouds would darken the early morning the next Sabbath day as he hurried to milk the cows. His family and all those from all over the plain of Shinar would soon gather in a large open space near Grandpapa Noah's home for their conference.

Thin, wispy clouds passed over the waning moon. The day would be sunny and bright.

Afra hurried to milk the cows and deliver it before quickly changing. He strode the short distance between his papa's and grandpapa's homes. The door opened, and Egypt stepped out. She wore her hair hanging loose over her shoulders across her best dress. It gleamed with a hint of auburn. He loved this look on her. She glanced up at the sky as he had.

"It will be a beautiful day," she said.

"Much like you," he said, kissing her gently on the mouth. He marveled at her warm lips. He was even more astonished that she would allow the kiss. He should have asked her to marry him much sooner.

They walked arm in arm as people streamed from all parts of the plain toward Grandpapa Noah's home and the altar built many years before when the smaller family settled on the plain.

When they arrived, they found a space near the front of the altar, close to where Grandpapa Noah would speak. Egypt produced two small cushions from her pocket for them to sit on. They sat near each other.

"I have worked hard on our home," Afra told Egypt.

"And I have discovered more jugs and dishes than I thought I had made. Some were cracked. I took them to the midden heap."

"We will have enough. Being with you is enough."

"What do you think Grandpapa Noa wants to tell us?" she asked.

"I do not know. It must be important for him to call everyone together. This is not a typical sacrifice day."

Soon the large space filled. Children ran along the edges of the crowd, weaving between those seated on the ground. Mamas and papas allowed them to run for a time. They would be sitting for a long time when Grandpapa Noah joined them.

The crowd quieted when Uncle Shem came out of the house with a chair. He set it in front of the crowd. The multitude quieted as Grandpapa Noah and Grandmama Imma left the house, supported by Uncle Shem, Uncle Japeth, and Grandpapa Ham. Grandpapa helped Grandmama to sit in the chair, then moved up the ramp a distance to be seen and hard by the vast crowd.

Children ran to their parents and everyone sat still, waiting to hear what he had to say. Afra took Egyptus's hand in his and gazed at his grandpapa.

Grandpapa spoke to them about the purpose and meaning of sacrifice, reminding them it was to point their minds to the coming sacrifice of Jehovah. He taught of the symbolism of the white ram Shem brought before sacrificing it.

As a warmth filled Afra, he knew Jehovah had accepted the sacrifice. Egyptus gripped his hand. Afra knew she felt the love of their God as he did. If Jehovah would give himself for them, He had a great love indeed.

They watched in awe as Grandpapa completed the sacrifice. Afterward, Grandpapa Noah spoke to them of the laws they had not obeyed as carefully as they should have. His calm face and voice belied the difficulty he expected.

Afra squeezed Egyptus's hand, telling her they would avoid the calamities Grandpapa predicted.

Grandpapa Noah continued. "Our family grows. For now, we are few enough we can continue to live in Shinar. But the time comes soon when we will be required to spread out on the land. Jehovah knows the challenges and the evil that comes when we confine ourselves to a small space. The earth is large. There is room for all to live without crowding together."

Afra glanced toward Egyptus. *Will she leave with me when it is time? Will she leave her mama?* She stared at their grandpapa and took a slow, deep breath.

"We think there is enough space for all the people here, but soon it will not hold us all." Grandpapa Noah swept his hand out toward the vastness of the plain. "The Destroyer steps in and encourages anger and hatred as we live closer together. We do not want this to happen. If you desire to explore with your family, come speak with me. I encourage you to spread out into other lands and valleys. This is a beautiful earth with many places for us to live."

Men rumbled among themselves. Many were happy in their homes. Afra had heard of a few who had asked permission to explore earlier and had not received it. How many would now hope to travel and explore.

"I wanted to explore to the west and across the mountains," Afra whispered. "Papa would not allow it. He said we are all needed here in Shinar."

Grandpapa Noah waited for the men to stop. "The problem with leaving this homeland is that many of you will leave Jehovah's protecting influence. You will forget Him. You will not have the right to sacrifice to Him. The Destroyer will entice you to worship gods of your own making, those he supports."

Grandpapa Noah stared out at the men and women of his family. "We face a dilemma, for we will fall to the Destroyer if we stay here and fill this valley with people, as certainly as many of your children will forget who brought them safely across the waters. They will believe you and me to be a myth, as people who lived before we entered the ark believed Adam and Eve were myths."

Afra heard some of his younger cousins mumble.

"They are not a myth?"

"Has anyone here seen or spoken to either of them?"

Egyptus shook her head. "I have read the words of Eve's book. I know how she lived."

"Some of you struggle even now to believe Adam and Eve lived, that they willingly left the garden so we would live. It is difficult to believe when Adam died. It was almost a hundred years before my birth. But my papa and grandpapas knew him. Each received a blessing from him."

"Can you believe it? How would it be to receive a blessing from Adam?" Afra whispered into Egyptus's ear.

"And to learn at Eve's feet," Egyptus murmured.

They returned their attention to Grandpapa Noah. "As time passes, you and I will become myths. We must teach our children to remember our parents and remember to honor and worship Jehovah."

Grandpapa Noah spoke words of encouragement before excusing the crowd.

After the rite, Egyptus and Afra met Uncle Shem, who Grandpapa Noah had honored.

Shem shook Afra's hand and kissed Egyptus on the cheek. "Papa says you two will soon marry?"

"If he ever completes our home," Egyptus said, winking at Afra.

"Homes take longer than we expect sometimes," Shem said. "Perhaps we can get some help for him."

"Would you?" Afra asked. "Papa and my brothers have helped, as have Egyptus's brothers, but we have all been busy with harvesting the grains. The cold comes soon."

"We need grain to feed us. I will ask around. Perhaps we can help complete your home before the rain falls."

"That would be wonderful," Afra said.

Two days later, Mama handed Papa a basket of food for his midday meal. He and other men of their large family rode in wagons, on horses, or marched to Afra's new home. Women soon converged on Egyptus's home bearing packages and baskets.

"With our men helping your Afra complete your new home, we decided to help you complete your preparations," Auntie Amina said.

The women sat on cushions they had brought with them or on the chairs Egyptus and Ruth dragged from the house. Grandmama Imma sat in a chair, joining in the laughter as women teased Egyptus. As guest of honor, Egyptus sat between her Mama and Grandmama Imma.

"We heard there were a few things you have not yet made for yourself," Auntie Edna said. "Since the men are at your new home getting it ready, we gathered gifts."

Auntie Edna handed Egyptus a package wrapped in a beautiful blanket. Egyptus unwrapped the blanket to find a big urn.

"I needed one of these," Egyptus cried, tears of gratitude pooling in her eyes.

Grandmama gave her a big cauldron for her laundry. Auntie Amina gave her a beautiful rug. Other women provided cooking pots, water urns, smaller urns, blankets, rugs, serving dishes, and many other useful and beautiful needed items for her new home.

"I thank you for your generosity," Egyptus said after she opened the last package. "We will have a beautiful home because of these gifts. We will always remember you."

The women opened other baskets and withdrew food. Egyptus rose to help serve, but Grandmama Imma pulled her back to her seat.

"This celebration is for you. Sit here and allow others to serve you. You can serve us another day."

"But ... This is my home," Egyptus argued. "I should serve my guests."

"But nothing," Grandmama replied. "You are our guest today. We are here for you."

Ruth brought water and juice from the storage. Egyptus wondered when they would celebrate her coming marriage. Each woman withdrew a cup from their pockets and Ruth and the other girls poured the drinks. As they sat back eating and drinking, the women told stories of their weddings and their men.

"My dress caught in the door as I entered the sanctuary," one woman said with a laugh. "It tore up much too far to be modest. Mama wrapped a colorful, light blanket around my waist, covering up the tear. Everyone thought I planned a colorful overskirt and complemented me on my style. Only mama and my man knew the skirt of my dress had torn so far."

"Is that why so many of our young women wear a colorful overskirt?" Auntie Amina asked. "I often wondered." She turned to Egyptus. "Are you planning to wear one?"

Egyptus shook her head and bit her lip. "No. I have nothing new to wear yet. We have been too busy with the harvest and threshing since Afra asked me to marry him. I have had no time to weave new fabric or sew a new dress."

"We suspected this would be a problem for you," Elva said. "Afra waited much too long to ask." She signaled to her daughters who jumped up and ran across the space to their home.

Not many breaths later they returned, carrying a basket between them.

"This is for you," Lili said, handing the basket to Egyptus.

Egyptus sat on her hands, amazed that they would give her more. "But you already gave me a beautiful gift."

"We want you to wear a beautiful new dress on the day you marry our brother," Lili said.

Egyptus opened the basket and pulled out a beautiful linen dress embroidered with local red and blue birds along the hems. "When did you have time to make this?"

"We knew Afra would ask you to be his wife eventually. We also knew he would not give you enough time to make a dress," Elva said. "So, we wove the fabric during the last cold time and cut it out and sewed it when we had time. We finished the dress last week, just before he finally asked you."

Egyptus leapt from her chair and threw her arms around Lili, then Elva and the other girls. "Thank you! I planned to wear my best dress. Now I can wear this lovely new dress."

"Put it on and show us," Mama said.

"Will you help me?" Egyptus asked.

They took the basket and dress inside, where Mama helped her pull the new dress over her head and tie it at her shoulders and waist.

Near the bottom of the basket, they found a rose-colored overskirt and a matching new pocket. Mama tied the skirt around Egyptus's waist and helped to put the new pocket over her shoulder.

"You wait here for ten breaths so you can come out alone," Mama said at the door. She hurried out to take her place with the other women.

Egyptus counted, as Mama suggested, then opened the door and stepped through. The women let out whispers of awe and clapped for her. She walked between them to show off the new dress. When she reached Elva, she hugged her. "I would never have something so nice without your help."

"I knew my Afra would not give you enough time to make a dress for yourself. I hoped you would like this one."

"I do. Thank you."

The other women turned to their neighbors to visit.

"I do not want to get this beautiful dress dirty before the day I wear it for Afra," Egyptus said. "Come with me to help me take it off, Elva."

The two women walked back into the house with fewer comments from the others. Several told her she looked beautiful and that she would be a beautiful bride.

As Elva helped her take the dress off, Egyptus shook her head. "I have been thinking. You have always been Elva to me, my brother's wife. What will I call you now? Should I call you Mama Elva like so many young brides?"

"That would be uncomfortable," Elva said. "We have always been Elva and Egyptus. Why would that change?"

"Because I am marrying your son?"

"Not enough reason to change our relationship. We will be closer now, not just the wife of your brother, but Canaan's wife, Afra's mama, and grandmama to your children." Elva gestured between herself and Egyptus. "Our bond will be tighter. You keep loving my son and I will always love you as sister and daughter."

Men swarmed over the little house Afra had started while the grains grew during the heat of the summer, each of them with an assignment. It did not take long to smooth the walls and build the fire spaces and floors. Men not working on the house went into the hills and brought back lengths of wood. These became tables, chairs, and other needed furniture.

They stopped at midday to open lunch baskets and share the food their wives and mamas sent with them. Many of them, especially his papa and brothers, teased Afra about waiting so long to ask for help.

"Men ask for help," Japheth's son, Elishah, said, holding a chicken leg in his big, gnarled hands.

"We do not allow our women to know, but we stand together to help, especially when a woman is waiting for a new home," Shem's son, Aram, said. He brushed back his flowing red hair.

"We are family," Shem added. "As family, we do our part to help others."

"Even when they wait forever to ask the woman they love to marry them," Jeb hooted.

Afra playfully punched his brother on the shoulder. "When you ask your woman, I will be there to help you." He glanced at the men sitting in small groups around him. "I will be here to help you all in any way you need. Call on me."

"Unless your wife needs you for something more important," Aram's son, Uz, teased. He shook back his red hair, that looked much like his papa's.

"I will remind her you helped me. She will understand," Afra said.

"Until it is time to give birth and you are off helping someone else," Uncle Cush said with a laugh. "That is a time you stay close to your woman. She needs you most then."

The men nodded, laughing softly, as they returned to their meals. *Those things happen? I had not considered them.*

Soon, the men stowed the remnants of their meals back in the basket, brushed off their tunics, and stretched, ready to return to their work.

Afra worked on covering the windows with wooden shutters, checking that they would open and close when necessary. They hung each shutter and ensured it worked properly by the time the sun dipped toward the western hills.

Stepping back from the house, Afra stared at his completed home filled with furniture. He had expected to take three or more weeks, even with his brothers' help. And now, these men had helped complete it, because he mentioned a need to the right person.

Shem gathered his tools and set them in his cart, preparing for the long ride across the plain to his own home. Afra hurried to speak with him before he urged his donkey to trot down the path.

"I thank you for organizing this for me," Afra said. "Egyptus would have needed to wait many weeks to have this fine home if only my brothers and I were working."

Shem's gentle smile warmed Afra in a way Papa Canaan had never done. "It was a pleasure to help a young man in need, especially to help you get your lovely young woman a home. Remember to help others when they are in need."

"You know I will," Afra said, setting his hand over his heart.

"I know," Shem said. He shook the reins and his donkey trotted away.

Afra watched for a long breath before turning to thank the other men as they walked past his new little gate and down the path toward their homes.

He turned around in time to see the evening sun bathing his home. Egyptus would love this home. And now they could marry.

"When will you ask Grandpapa Noah to perform your marriage rite?" Amor asked as the young men walked home behind all the other men.

"I could ask him to marry us tomorrow," Afra said.

"No!" Jeb cried. "We have a big hunt coming up. Wait until we have meat to share with the others for the wedding feast."

"Meat?" Afra asked, staring at Jeb. "But you two went hunting before we harvested the wheat. Why do we need more?"

"We have meat for the family, but not enough for a marriage feast. We will need more than we have."

Afra kicked at a clod in the road that broke into a cloud of dust. "I just want to be Egyptus's husband, to share our new home together."

"All men want that," Papa said, falling back to walk with Afra and his brothers. "But we need meat. Your woman can wait."

"When will it be a good time for our marriage rite?" Afra asked. *I want to be with Egyptus, forever, not just when we work together.*

Papa Canaan gazed into the darkening sky, thinking. "Next week. Grandpapa Noah will know."

Preparations

Even though the rain fell over the next few days, the men left to hunt wild animals while the women stayed behind, preparing their homes for Egyptus's wedding feast. Ruth and Hayam had decided to wait another month before their marriage.

In the evening, Egyptus sat with her mama and Ruth mending clothing.

"It is good the men have a barn to use to prepare and store all that meat they expect to bring home," Mama said. "We are working too hard to get our homes clean for them to drag their bloody animals through the house."

Ruth squirmed. "I do not like to see the animals after the men kill them."

"You like to eat their meat," Egyptus reminded her, stabbing her needle through the seam of a dress.

"I do, but their eyes are so sad."

"I remember the eyes of the animals in the ark," Mama said, her needle flying in and out of the seam she was repairing. "I remember the aurochs. If I remember correctly, after we bumped into a giant sea animal, the female was injured. Mama Imma called to me to come stitch her injury. The male stood above me, watching to be certain I would not hurt his mate. Light and intelligence filled their dark brown eyes. He cared for his mate."

"Gigantic animals like aurochs have light and intelligence?" Ruth asked. She bent to dig through the mending basket, searching for one of her dresses.

"The cows do," Egyptus said. "They know when we need to hurry and when we can take our time."

"All animals have intelligence," Mama said. "I learned that on the ark. They helped us in ways I would not have expected. After they left the ark, we did not see them regularly enough to recognize it. I suppose that is good, as we hunt them for food. I wonder if your papa and brothers will find an auroch on their hunt."

"Did the land change during the flood?" Egyptus asked. "It would be difficult for the animals to find their homes again if it had."

"It changed. Papa Noah tells us we landed in another part of the earth; one he had not traveled in the years he begged people to repent. No one has explored far in this land. The men found this plain and two other valleys when we searched for a new home. This was bigger, so we came here." Mama spoke with a wistfulness Egyptus seldom heard.

"Do you miss the old land?" Ruth asked. She lifted the dress she had searched for into her lap and threaded a needle.

"Sometimes I do. I sometimes would like to go back and see that little valley where your papa and I met. But it is not possible. That land, that home is gone." Mama's needle slowed.

"And those families?" Egyptus asked.

Tears brimmed in Mama's eyes, threatening to fall. "Yes. I sometimes think of them, how happy this place would make them. But they did not want it." Mama scrubbed her face with her hands. "We have you now. And you make us happy."

Egyptus and Ruth put their arms around their mama, pulling her close.

"Was there more that changed when you left the ark?" Egyptus asked, hoping to help ease the sadness from her mama's heart.

"The weather is different. We no longer receive long rainstorms lasting all day for many days. Our hot days are hotter. We now receive snow. We never had snow where we lived in the old world." Mama gently pushed the young women away and lifted the tunic to work on it once more.

"You never saw the snow?" Ruth asked, her mouth falling open as she retrieved the dress she worked on.

"I heard about it before, read about it even. Grandmama Ganet wrote about living in the mountains and the long snow. But we were limited to our small compound. We women could not leave, for our enemies sought to take us."

"Why would they do that?" Egyptus asked, once more stabbing the needle through the seam of the dress.

Mama touched the back of Egyptus's hand. "They thought they could force your Grandpapa Noah to stop preaching against their wickedness. We always stayed inside the walls of our compound unless we were with our men."

"I would love to see the old world you left behind," Ruth whispered. "Although not be required to stay within the walls of a compound."

"Not me," Egyptus said, searching the dress for more loose seams. "I am happy to have a little piece of land with a home, garden, and orchards ... and a few cows for milk, when Afra and I are married."

"You will be happy for now," Ruth said. "Someday you will want to leave."

"Are you a prophet now?" Mama asked, turning her stern face toward Ruth.

"No. I know Egyptus. She will want to explore and find a new home." Ruth did not look up from her mending.

"I may," Egyptus said with a small nod. "But not now. Now I look forward to the day when Afra and I can live together in our new home."

"Have you gone back to see Grandpapa Noah and set the day for your marriage rite?" Mama asked.

Egyptus set her mended dress aside and lifted the mending basket to her lap. "Not yet. He wanted to go yesterday, but the other men insisted they should leave for this hunting trip early in the morning. We plan to go see Grandpapa as soon as Afra returns."

"Consider your mamas as well," Mama said. "Elva and I will need a few days' warning to cook enough food for all the guests. Do not ask Grandpapa Noah to perform the marriage rite the day after the men return."

"I would not do that to you!" Egyptus cried, pulling a sleeping dress from the basket. "I know it takes time to prepare a wedding feast for our enormous family."

"You will want a day when it is dry. No one has a home large enough for everyone to crowd into," Ruth said.

"That is another problem," Mama said. "It is too bad we no longer have sanctuaries. We had a sanctuary in our village when I was young. It held everyone in the village for worship and special occasions."

"Someone should suggest to Grandpapa to build a sanctuary in each section of the plain," Ruth said, tying a knot in her thread.

"But even a smaller sanctuary would not be large enough to host all the members of our family." Egyptus threaded her needle once more and stabbed it into the torn seam of the sleeping dress. "Will we have to wait for the rain to stop before we can marry so everyone in this giant family can join us? That could be many months. And the rain already falls. The ground will be wet even on dry days."

"How can you tell in advance which day will be dry enough for everyone to gather?" Ruth asked. "I am grateful my Hayam works slowly on our home. We will plan our marriage rite after the storms end and before the earth dries enough to plant."

Egyptus allowed her sleeping dress to fall into her lap. "What will we do? I do not want to wait that long for our marriage rite."

"That is something you and Afra will have to decide, with the help of your papas and Grandpapa Noah," Mama said. "When Afra takes you to visit with Grandpapa, you can make those decisions. Grandpapa will know the right thing to do. He always does."

BEFORE EGYPT

Egyptus sat staring at the sleeping dress in her lap for several breaths before picking it up once more and finding her needle. "I can change nothing now. I will finish this mending so I can take an empty mending basket with me."

"Good plan," Mama said.

A week later, after the men returned from hunting and they had preserved all the meat they brought home, Egyptus pulled her cloak over her head to keep the rain off while she and Afra walked toward Grandpapa Noah's home.

"Will we have to wait for the rain to end before we can marry?" she asked.

"Why would we wait for the rain to end? We have a roof that holds out the rain." The question in Afra's voice almost caused Egyptus to giggle.

"So many people have helped us get ready for our marriage rite. All those men who helped you finish our home and all the many women who came that day and gave me beautiful gifts to use inside and meet our needs. They deserve to be part of the celebration."

Afra's frown seemed to reach the ground. "I want to be with you, only you. I do not want to wait for dry weather to accommodate a large crowd."

"And I want to be with only you, but ..."

Egyptus and Afra walked a distance in silence, dodging puddles and thinking of solutions to their problem.

"Is there a way we can have both?" Egyptus asked.

"How? The rains are here. Soon we will have snow. Where will we house all the people of Shinar?"

"Perhaps Grandpapa Noah will have an answer for us."

"Perhaps. But we should be able to solve this challenge. We will have many challenges like this, perhaps more challenging. We must

105

learn to come up with the answers without having to ask Grandpapa Noah each time. He will not always be with us." Afra stopped in the middle of the path. Rain beat on their hoods.

"We can find a way to include everyone and still do it soon," Egyptus said, glancing up at the rain. "What building is big enough everyone can fit inside out of this rain?"

They walked forward once more.

"We have homes ..." Afra said.

"Too small for everyone," Egyptus said.

"Sheds ..."

"Much too small."

"Barns ..."

"Those are bigger, but what would the animals do?"

"Storage barns ..."

"Filled with food." Egyptus wanted to jump into the puddles around her and forget this problem.

Afra's pace slowed. "There must be a way. If the wind is not blowing hard, we could build a shelter like we do for the animals when it is hot."

"Is there some way we can temporarily shelter the animals together, rather than giving each a home of their own?"

Egyptus watched Afra's closed eyes bounce as he considered the problem.

"We could do that, but only the cow barn is large enough for all the people in Shinar."

"And you use that barn every day to milk."

"And it smells like cows. We muck the manure out regularly, but it leaves a smell ..." Afra said, trailing off.

Egyptus waited, knowing he needed to chew on the thought.

"It would not be fair to the cows to take away their warm home. We need their milk. They stopped giving it for less before." Afra breathed out a heavy sigh. "How can we clean it enough for a feast and still use it for milking? I cannot see how."

Egyptus considered the buildings in their family compound. Homes, outbuildings, storage sheds, and barns. The threshing floor was large, big enough for many men to pound the wheat from the staves. They had threshed the wheat there even though it rained outside.

"What about the threshing floor? What do we store there now? Did you put the meat from your hunt there?"

"What?" Afra glanced up from the mud and scratched his cheek. "No. The walls do not reach the roof there."

"Is it big enough for a feast?"

Afra ran his hands through his hair as he considered the threshing building. "It should be dry enough. We may need to put screens near the top to block the wind if it is cold. That has more space than the barn."

"But more people will fit there. It has a roof and walls —"

"Of a sort," Afra agreed. "we could use that space. No animals would have to be displaced."

"And we would not need to wash and muck it out, nor smell the cows. Not all women like the smell as I do." Egyptus tucked her arm into Afra's elbow and laid her head on his shoulder.

He patted her hand. "It would be less work, if our papas agree. It is their threshing floor, your papa's threshing floor. Have you asked your parents how they plan to fit everyone in?"

Egyptus glanced up at Afra. "Ruth asked where we would put everyone. I suppose Mama and Papa are thinking about it. If we make the right suggestion ... Well, I thought they would see how able we are to live alone on the edge of the plain."

Afra squeezed her hand in his. "We can make the suggestion. I hope our papas accept it."

In front of them stood Grandpapa Noah's home glowed with a small light. "It looks like Grandpapa is waiting for us," Egyptus said.

"Why would he?"

"Grandpapa Noah always knows when we come to visit."

"Do you send a message ahead?"

"We never have," Egyptus said. "Grandpapa always knows."

Afra did not want to wait even one more day to become Egyptus's husband. Her concern for everyone else touched him, but he only wanted them married and together. Frustration bubbled through him.

Her suggestions were excellent, but it would mean more work for him and his brothers. Would they be willing to help him one more time? He silently huffed.

"Grandpapa Noah will know if we have a good plan," Egyptus said as they stepped onto his porch.

"It is your papa and mine I am concerned about — and my brothers. We are the ones who will need to make the threshing floor warm."

"And my sisters and I will clean and make it beautiful," Egyptus said.

Grandpapa Noah opened the door. "I thought someone would arrive soon."

Egyptus glanced at Afra. His frown moved to a grin.

"How do you always know?" Egyptus asked. "We never send word ahead, and you always know we are coming."

"I know. It comes to me."

Afra and Egyptus shook the rain from their cloaks and left them hanging on a peg inside the door. Grandmama Imma had a small rug below the pegs to absorb the dripping water.

He welcomed them into his home and invited them to sit in comfortable chairs. Grandmama Imma brought cups of warmed juice and sat with them.

"I heard you completed your home," Grandpapa Noah said. "Does that mean you are ready for your marriage rite?"

"We came to ask for a day and time when you can come perform the rite for us," Afra said, leaning forward.

"I am old. I do not know if I can travel to the edge of the plain to perform your rite there," Grandpapa said.

"We would not ask you to go that far," Egyptus said.

"No," Afra added. "We thought it would be good to use the threshing floor near Grandpapa Ham's home." He glanced into Egyptus's eyes in time to see a spark of joy.

"I understand you do not want to wait for the cold rain and snow to pass," Grandmama Imma agreed. "Would the threshing floor be warm?"

"With all those people?" Afra asked.

Grandpapa Noah chuckled. "Yes. People standing close warm things up."

"My brothers and I will enclose the top where it is open. That will keep the most of the cold and the wet out. It should be warm enough."

"And we, my sisters and I, will clean and make it beautiful," Egyptus said.

"You have been thinking about this," Grandpapa Noah said.

"We have. It is difficult to find a place for so many people to meet and feast," Afra said.

"Not everyone needs to observe the actual rite. It is a sacred ordinance. I can perform it here or in one of your parents' homes. Then they can have their feast on the threshing floor. That will keep the sweet words Father gave to us special."

"I did not think of that," Egyptus said. "It has been a while since we attended a marriage rite."

Grandmama Imma's eyebrows lifted. "Why is that? There have been many marriage rites in the heat of the summer."

Afra glanced at Egyptus. She shrugged.

"Perhaps we were busy with planting and harvesting. We did not receive invitations to those."

"Or your papas ..." Grandmama went silent.

"Refused to attend," Egyptus whispered with a small shrug.

"That is possible," Grandpapa Noah said. "When there are so many of us, sometimes others no longer know us as well. Our family is growing ever larger. I am certain there are cousins you have not yet met, even though they are your age."

"Perhaps. There are so many of them," Egyptus said.

Afra gripped her hand in his, seeking her support.

"And there are many younger cousins," Grandmama Imma added.

"Rather than invite all the people who live on the plains of Shinar, perhaps you could invite those who care about you, your family and friends," Grandpapa Noah suggested.

"Those who helped us finish our home," Afra said, speaking slowly.

"And the women who brought us gifts," Egyptus added. "That will fill our threshing floor, but it will not take so much from our storehouses."

Afra stretched his legs and crossed one over the other, sighing.

Egyptus glanced at him with her eyebrows raised.

"I can breathe once more. I feared after all the others have done to help me, we could not be married until the time it would have taken me to build our new home alone," he said.

"The important question for you remains," Grandpapa Noah said, gazing at Afra, then Egyptus. "When would you like me to perform the rite? I can do it here or in one of your parents' homes."

Afra gazed into Egyptus's eyes, trying to discern what she would want.

"Mama says not tomorrow," Egyptus said. "She and Elva need time to prepare the feast."

"That makes perfect sense," Grandpapa Noah said.

"And I do not want to wait even until tomorrow," Afra said. He winced as he said that aloud. *Did I say that? Yes. I do not want to wait.*

"I understand that as well," Grandmama Imma said. "Egyptus is a lovely young woman."

Afra glanced at her in time to see her skin glow a lovely shade of pink.

"Let me look at something." Grandpapa walked slowly to his desk and shuffled through sheets of velum. "Ah. There it is. Hmmm." He gazed at the pages. "Yes. What do you think about next week on the Sixth Day?"

Afra counted the days until the Sabbath. Three. Then six more days.

"Nine days," he muttered, staring at his fingers.

"And enough time to clean out and organize the threshing floor and for our mamas to prepare the feast," Egyptus whispered.

"Enough time to make and send out invitations to the families who will care enough to come," Afra added. "Will you help me write them?"

"I would love to do that," she said. "Will your brothers deliver them for us?"

"If they are not still busy working on the threshing floor and windows."

Afra heard a soft chortle. He glanced up to see Grandpapa Noah and Grandmama Imma covering their mouths with their hands.

"I remember planning like that ..." Grandpapa Noah said, grinning and stroking his long beard.

"Not for me," Grandmama Imma said. "You came and carried me away."

"I married you before I brought you to my home."

"True. And I will always be grateful you did."

Grandpapa Noah leaned close to Grandmama Imma and kissed her softly.

Afra grinned at Egyptus. "Someday that will be us," he whispered.

Home

E gyptus stood in her sleeping space, the remnants of her belongings packed carefully into a basket to be loaded into the cart after the celebration. She stared into the piece of polished copper hanging on her wall.

"Why does Afra love me? I am no beauty," she asked her reflection.

"Because you have the biggest heart I have ever seen," Mama said, pushing back the curtain that divided her space from the rest of the house. "Are you having second thoughts? It is not too late. Your Grandpapa Noah should arrive soon, but we can send him away."

"No, Mama!" Egyptus yelped. "I am happy to marry Afra. I love him. I sometimes wonder how he can love me. I can be a little pushy."

Mama's eyebrows lifted.

"I am often pushy. And my feet are big."

Mama set a basket by her feet and stepped to Egyptus to tie the ties at her shoulder.

"You two have been friends for so long. We have all waited for this day." She tied the overskirt around Egyptus's waist. "You are blessed to have sisters who love you so much. This is a lovely dress."

"Did you want to make my dress?" Egyptus asked. She glanced into her mama's eyes, fearing she would see that she had. "I can wear one you made."

"No, darling. You are beautiful in this dress and it took your sisters much effort to create it for you." Mama bent to open the basket at her feet and withdrew a circlet of dried flowers.

"These are for your head," she said, setting it gently on Egyptus's hair, careful not to muss it.

Egyptus gazed into the polished copper once more. "It is beautiful, Mama."

"Perfect for you." Mama lifted another item from her basket. "Turn," she ordered, making a spinning motion with her finger.

She obediently turned her back to her mama who carefully tied a string of old black and orange beads around her neck.

Egyptus fingered the beads. *Brown and orange beads? Where did these come from?* "Are these ...?"

"Yes, they are just like the ones Ziva wore. I found clay years ago and made these. I found them in a basket yesterday. They are not the ones Nat made so long ago for our grandmama, but they are like them. I want you to have them to remember that woman."

"And she suffered far away from her mama," Egyptus said, sniffing back tears.

"No tears," Mama ordered. "This is your marriage day. You should be happy."

"I am. Do you think Afra is?"

Afra stood outside the door to Grandpapa Ham's home breathing deeply.

Today is the day! I can finally claim Egyptus as my own, my love, my wife.

He pushed the air out of his lungs in a whoosh and breathed in once more. "Soon to be no more alone, but together with her for all time and forever. I cannot wait," he whispered.

"Then why are you standing here in the way?" Jeb asked, nudging him aside with an elbow.

"I suppose I am unsure."

"Of what? You love her. She loves you. You have a home to live in. What is there to be unsure of?"

"The future," Afra said. "What will the future bring us?"

Jed cackled as he pushed Grandpapa Ham's door open. "It will bring us life."

Life! Life together with Egyptus!

Afra followed his brother through the door. The excitement whirling through the room caught him up.

"You are here," Grandpapa Ham said, pounding him on the back. "I feared you would run away."

"Not me," Afra replied.

The door opened again and others entered. Soon the room filled with family. Grandpapa Noah entered from a back room.

"Are we ready for this?" he asked.

"I am," Afra said. "Where is Egyptus?"

"Here." Egyptus stepped from behind her tall brothers.

Afra's breath caught at the sight of her. "Stunning," he whispered. The dress, the circlet of flowers adorning her hair, the orange and black beads laying against her smooth skin all joined in perfection.

He lifted a hand to her. She floated across the room, taking his hand and staring lovingly into his eyes.

Love. This is our future.

"Are we ready?" Grandpapa Noah asked.

Afra and Egyptus knelt in front of him and nodded. Afra gripped her hands as Grandpapa spoke the sacred words that joined them for eternity. Jehovah blessed their marriage. He would bless them and their family as long as they remembered Him.

Many hours later, Egyptus and Afra quietly slipped away from the laughter and joy that filled the threshing floor. They kissed as they stepped into the crisp, late afternoon air.

"You are mine," Afra said, kissing her hungrily.

"And you are mine, forever," Egyptus said, returning his kiss. Heat surged through her body.

Afra pulled himself away. "Home. We must go home."

He mounted the horse his brother had saddled for them. Egyptus took his hand and let him pull her up behind him.

"Home," she breathed in his ear.

He guided the horse down the path and out the gate. Soon he nudged the horse into a run. They laughed together as they flew across the land.

Excitement filled Egyptus. She had married her best friend and the man she loved.

Afra pulled on the horse's reins. It came to a stop in front of their door. Afra slid off and turned to catch her.

"Welcome home," he said, holding her in his arms like a small child. His warmth and comfort surrounded her.

"Home." The word filled Egyptus with warmth and joy. "Our home."

Acknowledgments

Books are interesting things, coming from the mind of someone pecking at the keyboard, sharing stories from their minds. I am happy to have written another one!

I thank you, my reader, for staying all the way through this with me. You are amazing.

I give thanks to the many people who have helped me in this current journey:

-The ladies in my ANWA chapter have supported and encouraged me when I thought I had finished writing all there was for me to write.

- My husband who waits patiently for me to finish hiding in my office clicking the keys, and answering my silly questions.

-My parents who give me love and support, especially dad who at 95 is my best reader and proofreader.

-My AngelCast team who helped find the last mistakes and typos so this is easier to read.

-Julia Allen, my editor, who cleaned up the remnants of my Covid Brain and helped me resolve some problems.

-Dar Albert, who creates the most beautiful covers.

Thank you to you all, and especially you, my reader. I wouldn't be here without you.

Also By

ANGELIQUE CONGER

Before Egypt
Discovery
Settlement
Enemies
Women of the Covenant
Sarah, Mother of Nations
Hagar, Mother of Sorrows

About Author

Angelique Conger discovered the wonders of writing books later in her life. Books, however, have always been important to her. As a little girl in a small town, she was given her own library card at the tender age of five, highly unusual in those days.

Angelique reads a book, or three at once, much of the time. She reads most genres of books and until a few years ago only toyed with writing them. Since beginning, she has spent many hours each day learning the craft of writing and editing.

Many would consider Angelique Conger's books Christian focused, and they are because they focus on early events in the Bible. She writes of a people's beliefs in Jehovah. However, though she's read in much of the Bible and searched for more about these stories, there isn't much there. Her imagination fills in the missing information, which is most of it.

Angelique lives in Southern Nevada with her husband, a Simese cat named Sparky, and a new tuxedo kitten named Spicy.

Into Egypt: Discovery

I Must Leave

Why were these women screaming insults at her? Egyptus could not believe this was happening to her. She had done nothing to them. They should be comforting her. She still mourned the loss of her husband only seven weeks earlier. Yet, they shouted at her.

Afra had joined his brothers on a hunt for wild animals to feed their large family. His brothers had brought him home, shredded by the claws of a lion. He had lived only long enough to warn Egyptus she should leave their home on the plains of Shinar.

Egyptus had gathered together her sons and their wives and children, making plans to leave, although she did not understand his warning.

Now she knew.

"Adulteress!" Niva cried. "You look upon my husband to take him as your man."

"I do not!" Egyptus cried. "I care only for my Afra, whom we buried. You stood beside me and wept with me."

"And now you seek my husband to comfort you. I saw you speaking to him."

"Yes, I spoke to Ludim. I asked his opinion, he is the son of my brother, as you know."

"You were standing too close to him. I could not see any space between you. And he had his arms around you."

Egyptus rolled her lips inward, then let them fall out. "He saw my sorrow. Afra was my best friend. It is hard to live without him."

"Exactly!" Niva cried. "You miss your husband and now try to take mine into your bed."

"I want nothing to do with your husband. He is the son of my brother. Why would I want him in my bed? I want no man but Afra."

Other women, Niva's friends, gathered round, screaming horrid words at Egyptus.

"You had better not be near my husband."

"Stay away from my man."

"No woman can trust a woman whose husband died. You are not trustworthy."

They surrounded Egyptus. Women pounded their fists against her arms, back, and body. Her screams brought others to join in the beating. When she fell, they kicked her in the stomach until she curled up, protecting it, with her hands over her head.

"What is going on here?" a man's voice boomed.

"She tries to take our men."

"We give her what she deserves."

"She does not belong here among decent women."

"Who do you accuse of her such terrible things?" the man asked.

His voice sounded vaguely familiar, but between the kicks and the shouting, she could not make out why.

Egyptus heard the women's voices move away. Still, she held her tight protective position. One woman darted in and kicked her in the back.

"Stop that," the man cried. "No one deserves for you to kick and beat them."

Women continued to surround her, murmuring curses and threats. The man bent to her, gently pulling her hands from her head.

"Egyptus?" her papa asked.

"Is that you, Papa?" she whimpered, staring through an eye that did not want to open.

"What have they done to you?" he turned to the other women. "This is my daughter. Has she not been through more than any of you could imagine? Her Afra is one of the first bodies buried in our sad little burial ground? You should all be ashamed."

"She looks at our men. I saw mine embracing her," Niva's shout carried the feral sound of a wild animal.

"Why would she want your husband? She misses Afra's manliness."

Niva's harrumph echoed off the nearby building. Egyptus grinned, but it hurt.

Papa bent over and lifted her into his strong arms like he had when she tripped over a rock when she was little. Egyptus lay her head against his shoulder.

"You do not fear Mama will accuse me of attempting to steal her man?" Egyptus asked, only half teasing.

"No. Her anger with those other women will cause great fear." Papa carried her across the central open space in front of a square of homes.

Egyptus closed her eyes and rested in his strength. No one would hurt her when Papa Ham held her close like this.

He stomped up the stairs and opened the door. "Baysa, our girl needs some attention," he called.

"Our girl? Which one? Why?" Mama said, entering the living space where the family welcomed visitors. "Oh, Egyptus! What happened?"

Papa carefully set her on a long seat. "I came upon a circle of women screeching and attacking something in the middle of them. Imagine my surprise when I discovered our Egyptus as the object of their anger."

"Egyptus? Why would they do that?" Mama brushed Egyptus's hair back off her face. "Wait to tell me. I will get something for those bruises."

Papa went with Mama and Egyptus lay her head back, closing the one eye that would open.

Why did they attack me? I grieve for Afra. I care nothing for other men. Why would they hate me for losing him?

Mama bustled in with a bowl and a cloth, followed by Papa's heavier steps. Egyptus listened to the cloth fall into the bowl and the water wring out of it. Mama's gentle hand set the cool cloth smelling of nettle on her eye.

"This should take some of the bruising and swelling from your eye. Do you have other bruises?"

"It would surprise me if she did not. They punched and kicked her to the ground, then kept beating her. I found her curled into a ball with her hands over her head. Too many fought against her for her to fight back."

"Did you not fight back?" Mama's voice oozed concern.

Egyptus opened her one good eye. "There were too many to fight back. I tried to tell Niva I have no desire to take her man, or any other woman's man. I only want my own man." Tears leaked from her closed eye. "Why did that lion have to attack my Afra?"

"You will have to take that question to Jehovah," Papa answered. "They say he stood on the edge of the group, protecting the younger men. They saw the lion and tried to move out of her territory before she attacked."

"But why would she attack? Why my Afra?" Egyptus lifted her head from the seat.

"Kits? Most mamas will attack to protect their little ones. She may have kittens."

"Oh. That makes more sense. They must have come between the mama lion and her babies."

"Perhaps. The men brought him home for help as soon as they could."

"Still too late. Her scratches cut him up. I feel like those women were the lioness attacking me. I hurt everywhere."

Mama sent Papa out for some aloe, then lifted Egyptus's dress. "Oh, Egyptus. They were angry. But you did nothing to deserve all these bruises."

"And the pain in my ribs? I suspect their kicking broke them."

Mama touched her ribs. Egyptus moaned.

"I suspect you are correct. Those ribs could be broken. You will hurt for some time."

Mama spread a light blanket over her body, except her back.

Papa entered the room with a fresh leaf of aloe. "Look at those bruises," he cried.

"Papa!" Egyptus said, grabbing the blanket close.

"I saw you as a newborn babe. I am your Papa."

"And I am a grandmama. It is not right."

Papa gave Mama the aloe and moved away, to protect Egyptus's dignity. "Did they miss any part of your body?"

"They only kicked me in the stomach twice before I curled inward. They took out their anger on my back, legs, and head."

"I can tell."

Papa sat in a seat close enough to squeeze the oozing center from the aloe leaf for her mama, and still allow Egyptus privacy. Egyptus lay accepting her ministrations. Mama's hands soothed her fears, allowing her to relax.

"Afra spoke the truth before he died," Egyptus mused when Mama had washed and covered almost all her bruises with the cleansing wash and the aloe gel.

"What did he tell you?" Papa asked.

"He said I would have to leave this place and find another home. I did not understand. I thought followers of Jehovah would have compassion for one who lost her husband." Egyptus shook her head slightly and moaned. "The women have none. They all think I want their man. Ugh. None could match my Afra."

"They see a woman without a man," Basya said. "In their insecurity, they fear their man will comfort you and find them wanting."

"I want none of it. My sons and I will leave tomorrow."

"Not tomorrow, Egyptus," Papa said.

"And why not?" Egyptus demanded.

"Tomorrow is the Sabbath. Wait a day."

Do you want to read more? Go to Into Egypt: Discovery[1].

---

1. https://angeliquecongerauthor.com/mybooklinks/2286132

Don't miss out!

Visit the website below and you can sign up to receive emails whenever Angelique Conger publishes a new book. There's no charge and no obligation.

https://books2read.com/r/B-A-NFPH-MGZOC

BOOKS 2 READ

Connecting independent readers to independent writers.

www.ingramcontent.com/pod-product-compliance
Lightning Source LLC
Chambersburg PA
CBHW070040030726
47506CB00003B/811